In the Name of God

Yasmina Khadra

IN THE NAME OF GOD

TRANSLATED BY
Linda Black

The Toby Press

First published in Great Britain 2000

Reprinted 2002

The Toby Press *Ltd, London*
www.tobypress.com

Originally published as *Les agneaux du Seigneur*
Copyright © Editions Julliard, Paris 1998

Translation copyright © Linda Black 2000

ISBN 1 902881 06 0 (C)
ISBN 1 902881 11 7 (PB)

A CIP catalogue record for this title is available from the British Library

Designed by Fresh Produce, London

Typeset in Garamond by
Rowland Phototypesetting Ltd, Bury St Edmunds

Printed and bound in the United States by
Thomson-Shore, Inc., Michigan

The author chose to use a number of Arabic words which the translator has retained. A Glossary is provided on pp. 213–15.

Part 1

Chapter one

The sun was retreating behind the mountain. A few blood-stained streaks tried in vain to cling to the clouds. They dispersed and melted into the encroaching darkness. At the foot of the hill, the village was preparing to go to earth. In the narrow, winding streets, the noises had died down. Only a band of urchins swarmed like hornets, scouring every nook and cranny.

Kada Hilal contemplated his cigarette, engrossed in thought. Whenever he opened his mouth to say something, his neck would just droop down a little further and only a sigh would escape him.

Beside him, Jafer Wahab noticed that his hands were raw from tugging his shoelaces. He leaned against a carob tree, let his gaze wander over the fields, and then wearily closed his eyes in the hope of shutting out the all-pervasive despondency around him.

"Why don't you come with me to Sidi Bel Abbes?" suggested Allal Sidhom.

"What for?"

"I'll have a word with my boss. He's accommodating."

Jafer gave a faint smile.

"I'm not educated enough for a job in the police."

"The police isn't the only option."

"Don't bother. I'm a good-for-nothing. Anyway, I don't think I could live far from this wretched village."

"You're right," agreed Kada, resignedly. "This place is our only true village, and our only homeland is our family. Allal's a cop. He's changed camp. He doesn't see things through his own eyes any more, but through *theirs*."

"You're talking rubbish," retorted Allal.

"You're like modern women, if you want my opinion. You think you're liberated, but you've just become a joke. I too used to think this huge country belonged to me. After truanting for two years, I realized I was going round and round in circles, like a screw whose thread has worn away. So I came back. True, nothing ever happens around here, only at least we are among our own kind . . . Jafer won't go anywhere. He'll stay here, and this is where he'll die. The damned rain will eventually take pity on us, our crops will grow again, we'll have food and water, and enough to get away from this cursed land that insists on ignoring us."

Kada Hilal angrily swatted a fly. His jaws clenched for a moment before beginning to work up and down in his permanently enraged face. The great-grandson of a tyrannical *caid*, his upbringing had been austere, and he despised the new ruling classes whose greed had swallowed the greater part of his inheritance. Reduced to the rank of a "commoner", Kada could not forgive the daily humiliation. From his earliest infancy he had dreamed of regaining his dignity and privileges in a village that was in continual decline. Tired of the struggle, he had become a primary schoolteacher out of resentment, and his ever-swelling hatred drove him to join the still clandestine Islamist movement.

He turned to the policeman, his eyes blazing.

"You think you're successful, Allal. Others before you did, too, and shouted it from the rooftops. Then they came back disillusioned to loaf around here, but they didn't get any sympathy."

"That's rubbish . . ."

"Oh is it? At first, people are like mules, on with the blinkers, and off they rush. They have only one thing in mind: to get the hell out of here. But they return to square one. And then it's too late to change tack. That's what happened to my uncle, the deputy. He considered himself an authority. Result: he ended his life talking to the trees in the forest, because nobody cared to listen to him. Watch out, Jafer. Allal's a cop, you can't trust him any more."

"I wasn't born yesterday," grumbled Jafer looking hurt.

Allal noticed that his branch was broken. He wiped his clammy hands on his knees and contented himself with watching Zane-the-dwarf perched like a bird of prey on a branch, on the other side of the river.

The scent of the trees and shrubs grew stronger. Down below, the village huddled in the shadows. The brats had disappeared. The incongruous braying of a donkey rang out over the countryside and was quickly drowned out by the yapping of dogs.

Kada chain-smoked. His face was inscrutable, as hard to fathom as his sulking.

"When I try to take stock of my life," said Jafer, "I find it's worthless. Twenty-seven empty years. Days as blank as the nights. You get up in the morning and go to bed at night, numb with boredom. Always the same reflexes, the same trivialities . . ."

"You don't make any effort to change things, either," Allal criticized.

"What can I do?" retorted Jafer heatedly. He was known in the village for doing as little as possible. "If I'd had the choice, I'd have been a lion. Not to be king – being a king's too much trouble – but just having it nice and cushy, being a pimp when he feels like it, with a harem, a load of kids, the scent of the kill and an outlandish sense of impunity . . ."

"Shall I tell you something?" protested the policeman. "A man who dreams of being an animal doesn't deserve to live. If you really want to make something of your useless life, learn to come to terms with yourself."

"What does coming to terms with yourself mean?"

"It means not trusting a cop," grumbled Kada.

"Yeah," replied Allal with mounting irritation. "You sit there twiddling your thumbs waiting for the Lord to send Gabriel to fan you with his wings."

The muezzin's cry rang out. Kada mechanically stubbed out his cigarette on a rock, dusted himself down and raced down the slope.

"See you after prayer?" called Allal.

"Maybe."

"We'll be at my place."

Kada made a vague gesture and vanished behind the trees.

The horizon was growing dark, as if a storm were gathering. In a few moments, the village, the mountain, the whole world would be plunged into night. The little villages in the distance looked like Christmas trees. A breeze rippled through the leaves and rustled the grass, trying to soothe the woods exhausted by the scorching heat. The local dogs began their howling to locate each other in the half-darkness, and the hill, gloomy for a moment, was drowned in the chirring of the forest.

"I've got a bottle of wine at home," proposed Allal.

Jafer nodded his head. A laugh rang out, short and nervous. After considering things at length, he suddenly clapped his hands.

"How about going to see Mammy-the-whore?"

"My car's broken down."

"We'll take a taxi."

"How will we get back? Anyway, we promised Kada we'd meet him at my place."

"He won't come."

"He will."

Jafer grasped his friend's wrist, pleading:

"Your leave's nearly over. You know I can't face up to a whore if you're not with me."

"Not this evening. Besides, Mammy only sees people by appointment."

Jafer relaxed his grip. Once more, he was overwhelmed by world-weariness.

Allal Sidhom's house was at the edge of the village, hidden among prickly pear trees. It was a shack with a crumbling façade, a solid iron door and a neglected patio ill-lit by a street lamp. Allal lived there with his mother, a furtive widow, and his two sisters whose bloom had long faded.

The two friends made themselves comfortable in one of the rooms, one sitting on a upholstered seat and the other on a stool. Faded curtains attempted to minimize the ugliness of the walls, while a naked bulb struggled to cast its light through the fly specks coating it. On a rudimentary bedside table was a portrait of Allal, looking resolute in his policeman's uniform. Jafer stared at the photo for a moment before turning it round with a mysterious gesture which did not escape the policeman's notice.

"You've got a house, an income and a career . . . when are you going to get round to taking a wife?"

"Let's say that my beloved hasn't yet reached the requisite age," replied Allal.

"Have you got your eye on someone?"

"Both eyes."

"Is it a secret?"

"Perhaps . . ."

Jafer rose from the stool and went to join Allal on the bench.

"You're thinking of the mayor's daughter, aren't you?"

"I can't keep anything from you."

"Sarah would never give up her comfort for a hovel like yours."

"What do you know?"

Jafer didn't look too pleased. Sarah was like the Vestal Virgin of Ghachimat. There wasn't a single young man in the village who didn't dream about her.

"A lot of guys will be envious," he muttered.

"You for a start."

"You don't stand a chance."

"What is chance?"

Jafer didn't answer. He gazed at the policeman's handsome face, his finely shaped moustache and disarming smile, his clear eyes with their hint of anxiety. At twenty-six, Allal still had a boyish air and that indefinable quality that made his presence comforting and his absence unbearable.

"Let's have a sniff of that bottle, shall we?"

Later, Kada the schoolteacher found them slumped on the seat, drunk.

"Have you heard the latest?" burbled Jafer. "Our cop is planning to steal Sarah from us."

The schoolteacher frowned. He said nothing. He merely lay down on a mat and stared at the ceiling, a strange glint in his eyes.

Chapter two

Issa Osmane scratched the huge nose that consumed his face. The bones at the back of his neck jutted out even more under the mayor's harsh gaze. Behind the counter stood the café owner, his turban unravelled. He and his customers waited with bated breath for the mayor's wrath to descend on this clerk who was loathed by the entire village.

Issa had collaborated with the SAS during the war, when he was the only Arab to frequent the French soldiers' mess. True, he hadn't grassed or beaten up his own people, but he thought only of filling his own belly while others were dying of hunger and gall. At the end of the war, the *maquisards* had confiscated his belongings and decided to crucify him in the square. If it had not been for the intervention of the revered Sidi Saim, his corpse would have rotted on the river bank.

At Ghachimat, the collective memory fed on rancour.

Now, Issa was paying. His clothes stank. He rarely had enough to eat. He hugged the walls when he walked, like the silhouette of a shadow puppet, keeping his head down and making himself very small. In Ghachimat, when a man was desperate to the point of abandoning his faith, he would see the "traitor" grovelling, and suddenly his own will to live would be re-kindled.

The mayor was trembling with rage. He thumped the table, hammering home his threats.

"If you don't bring me the key in five minutes, Issa you dolt, I'll rip the hide from your back with my bare hands. Yesterday you lost my bag, and today the town hall will be closed because of your stupidity . . ."

Issa wretchedly smoothed the threadbare collar of his jacket.

"What are you waiting for?" bellowed the mayor.

The old man jumped, then backed away, terrified, and ran off as if possessed.

"He's too old," said the imam Salah from the next table. "Already, when he was young, he wasn't all there. Why don't you fire him?"

"And who'd run my errands?" retorted the mayor, exasperated. "I've got responsibilities, I can't be in two places at the same time."

"Hire somebody else."

The mayor curled his lip in an angry scowl:

"People prefer to moulder at the foot of a tree rather than make themselves useful for once. There, look at them," he added, pointing contemptuously at the peasant farmers seated at nearby tables. "They have no other ambition than to substitute themselves for the chairs they're sitting on."

The farmers hid behind their cups. The mayor looked them up and down, then he straightened up, flung the ends of his burnous over his shoulders and roared:

"One day, they'll have to be evicted from here with a bulldozer. They're champions when it comes to having children, but when it comes to feeding them . . ." he pointed skywards, "they leave that to God. Do you know, most revered imam, why it is that each year our fields are more and more overrun with brambles and stones?"

The imam nodded sympathetically.

The mayor raised his arms in a damning gesture and stomped out in a fury. The café-owner began to polish the counter. The tables soon began to creak once more under the aggression of the domino players.

Tej Osmane wiped his hands on a rag hanging out of the back pocket of his trousers and shut the bonnet of the Peugeot. Just then his father, Issa, ran past the garage, the corners of his mouth foaming.

"Now what's happened?" shouted the son.

Issa was in too much of a hurry to stop. He waved awkwardly as he headed towards his hovel at the end of the alleyway.

Tej puffed out his cheeks and heaved a sigh.

On the other side of the road, opposite the garage, Hadji Maurice was slumped in a wicker chair, his face crimson, a large fan in his hand. At the age of eighty, Hadji Maurice expected nothing more out of life. So he exercised himself by idling away the time. When criticized for his excessive laziness, he would reply: "I'm turning Arab", and that was enough to shut people up. Maurice had once worked as steward for the Xaviers. He was enterprising, uncomplicated, honest with his employers and polite to the seasonal workers. After Independence, following repeated intimidation and threatening letters, and the massacre of the *harkis*, he had quickly grabbed a few undershirts and left for France, a country completely unknown to him. He was depressed by the perpetual greyness of Lyon. It was a horrid, noisy city, where you rarely met the people who lived in the neighbouring apartment. He soon began to miss the sunshine of his native land and the spontaneity of the *fellahin*. Unable to stand the homesickness any longer, he took his courage in both hands, boarded the first steam ship and returned to Ghachimat where the sound of the shepherds' flutes was sweeter than the blackbird's song, where the human warmth was like that of no other place on earth. His "rehabilitation" demanded massive concessions. Maurice had a series of jobs: builder, night-watchman, underling then primary schoolteacher. He married a Muslim woman who did not bear him any children but excelled in making him forget the fact. When his reflexes became dulled, he received a pension and began to let himself go, living at his own lethargic pace. With age, he had become fat and wise, and it was with infinite pleasure that he had discovered the unutterably sweet joys of idleness.

"Come and have a glass of tea with me, Tej."

The mechanic consulted his watch, then went and squatted before the old man. Hadji Maurice fanned himself to cool his streaming jowls.

"Is your pump working all right?"

"Wonderfully," replied the old man. "And to think that moron Slimane nearly wrecked it. What's more, he expected me to pay him. What does he take me for, the Good Samaritan?"

Tej unearthed a stone, weighed it and put it back in its hole. His voice trembled:

"I was very grateful for your intervention, the other day."

"Bah!" said the old man. "People aren't really bad. It's poverty that is. Your father never harmed a fly. I remember how when a farmer was fired, he always managed to find him another job. Unfortunately, people only remember what suits them."

"I just wanted to tell you."

"You have. No need to say another word."

Hadji Maurice looked up and followed the aerobatics of a pair of sparrows. Tattered clouds stubbornly broke up over the permanently whitish, barren mountains. On the hillside, a flock of sheep grazed in the dust, while a young shepherd dozed on a rock, overcome by the heat.

Tej put down his glass on seeing his father tearing up the street waving a key.

"I've found it! I've found it!"

He ran past his son, gasping for breath, delirious, his eyes bulging with an absurd, radiant joy, akin to deliverance. Hadji Maurice looked away out of a sense of decency. Tej went back to his workshop, put away his tools and set a wheel in motion at the back of the garage. His gestures suddenly exuded mute rage.

"Well, scrap merchant," said Jafer coming up behind him, "is our cart ready yet?"

Tej swung round. Behind Jafer, Allal the policeman and Kada the schoolteacher raised their hands in greeting.

"I've fixed it."

"What was it?"

"Dirt in the carburettor."

"How much do I owe you?"

"Forget it. It was a pleasure."

Allal insisted, and slipped a note into his pocket. In the end, the mechanic accepted. He took Kada's arm, took him discreetly to one side and told him:

"Sheikh Abbas was released from gaol this morning."

"I know. We're going into town. Do you need anything?"

The mechanic thought:

"If you're going to the Grand Mosque, try and get me the book I told you about."

Allal revved up the engine, to the delight of Jafer sitting beside him. Kada leapt onto the back seat.

As they left the village, Jelloul-the-fool stood to attention on catching sight of the Peugeot and gave a military salute. The car climbed an embankment and roared off down the track, raising a huge cloud of dust. Allal drove past the mayor's house. Sarah was there, sitting in the garden with her mother. The three friends swivelled round to look at her, but her azure gaze picked out that of the policeman. The three young men all shivered, taking care not to venture words that might betray their innermost thoughts.

Chapter three

Ramdane Ich was happy. His son Abbas had come back.

People were flocking to his patio, bearing gifts. He allowed them to lay their heads on his chest, and at times permitted them to kiss his head. His cousins stood beside him, already disdainful, indifferent to the hypocritical joy of those who had been loath to share their grief the day the gendarmes had come to arrest their boy. Ramdane had not forgotten either. But seeing people prostrate themselves at his feet filled him with such conceit that he deigned to show indulgence. He had told Issa Osmane to slaughter seven curly-horned rams and had brought in the best cooks in the region so that the return of his son would remain etched in their memories for ever.

"It is a blessed day," declared the imam Salah, hugging

Ramdane close to him. "Where is our dear child? I'm longing to greet him."

And Ramdane, with that arrogance that only short-lived heroes are capable of, replied:

"He's resting in his room. He mustn't be disturbed."

The mayor himself had come, with his usual entourage. For once, he did not insist on being placed above everyone else, as was customary, and willingly removed his shoes before joining the notables in the sitting room.

In the next room, Hadji Mabrouka was playing the expiatory victim. The women crowded round, comforting her.

"Come on, Hadji, your son is back with you now."

The mother wallowed in her tears. She forced grief to the point of fainting from time to time. Streaks of mascara lined her face, and her hair, carefully piled up that morning, escaped from her headscarf and fell limply onto her heaving shoulders.

"Let her pour out her heart and rid it of the gall that nearly killed her," a huge matron commanded the swarm of women clustered around the weeping mother.

Ramdane was suddenly overcome by his wife's choking sobs and the interminable expressions of sympathy. He told his cousins to take charge of the party and asked his guests to excuse him for a moment.

"You're forgiven," they assured him. "We *understand.* Go on."

Outside, a crow flew across the sky, cawing. Its shadow glided over the uneven ground and was engulfed by that of the cacti.

Sheikh Abbas was a young man of twenty-five. His

frequent spells in prison had given him a messianic look. He was lording it at the back of the room, sitting cross-legged on some cushions, a profound look in his eyes and a string of worry-beads in his hands. His flock were jostling each other around him, silently cocooning this charismatic individual who had remained unbroken by the gaols of the *taghout*. Sheikh Abbas was the youngest imam in the region. At seventeen, he was already officiating in the most renowned mosques, displaying a tremendous knowledge and expounding a rhetoric that left the most skilful orators speechless. He was better able than anyone else to combine the Hadiths with citations from the poets. When he harangued corrupt officials and politicians' henchmen, his inflammatory words alone were almost enough to immolate them. Rumour had it that he had managed to convert all the thugs languishing behind bars.

For ordinary mortals, Sheikh Abbas was a sign from heaven. If he did not bring the Message itself, he was still its worthy servant. At least that was what the guests told themselves as they tucked into the couscous, sauce dribbling down their chins and little strings of meat caught between their teeth.

Sheikh Abbas did not eat. He sat on his throne, magnificent in his restraint, and watched his flock graze with a rare serenity.

"Didn't they beat him up?" asked Zane-the-dwarf between two hastily swallowed mouthfuls.

"You don't beat up a saint," retorted a colossus, his frenzied fingers demolishing a leg of lamb. "Sheikh Abbas is a spirit. No hand can harm him, no chain restrain him."

The dwarf realized that his indiscretion had cost him

his portion of meat. He immediately attacked the next tray.

Tej Osmane, the son of Issa-the-disgrace, was not eating either. Since he had managed to fight his way to the Sheikh's side, he was jealously guarding his place. They all wanted to be close to Abbas. He knew that a lot of people already resented him for this "sacrilege". He made himself very small to avoid the outraged looks that were growing increasingly venomous.

Each time the Sheikh moved, his entourage froze, on the alert for an order or a gesture. Abbas said nothing, A few friends were clowning around in the hope of wresting a smile from him. In vain. From time to time, however, he would make a show of allowing his gaze to fall on one of the jesters, and that was enough to make everybody happy.

"I'm so sorry to have to go," said Allal the policeman, wiping his hands on a tea towel. "My leave's over. I've got to be off early in the morning."

The Sheikh observed a moment's silence, as if he did not understand, and then said affably:

"Thank you for coming."

"I wish I could stay longer . . ."

"Of course. I was glad to see you again. Before you leave us, allow me to give you a present."

The Sheikh barely had time to clap his hands before 'Smail, a burly cousin, hurriedly handed him a box neatly wrapped in glittering paper.

"This is a Koran," explained the Sheikh. "A rare edition. It was made by an eminent craftsman in Mecca."

The policeman took the book with infinite precaution and rose.

"Allal Sidhom," added the Sheikh, "I've been thinking about you lately. You are a good lad. I value your honesty."

Allal made his farewells and left the room, with Jafer at his heels. Outside, darkness had swallowed up the mountain. The alleyways were empty, haunted by a few mangy dogs.

"He blessed you," Jafer congratulated him. Rarely had Abbas addressed the children of the *douar* in that way.

"We've always respected each other."

"I thought you were going back on Tuesday."

"I've been recalled. Seems it's urgent."

"I'm going to miss you."

"Find yourself a job."

"Don't start that again, please."

Allal stopped to scrutinize his friend.

"Imbecile. When will you get used to the idea? Try to stop looking so miserable and go back to the Ichs' place, or they'll think you have no regard for their son."

The policeman walked off. His shadow was immediately obscured by the darkness. Jafer stood there for a moment, listening to the dust crunching under his friend's footsteps before returning reluctantly to the Ichs' house.

Sarah could vaguely distinguish the muezzin's call amid the warbling of the birds. Her huge eyes opened wide, her beautiful face drowsy. Suddenly, she remembered something, jumped out of bed and rushed to the window. Without drawing the curtain, she gazed out.

A cock with a magnificent crest drew himself up on top of a fence. His crow carried far, stirring up the darkness. At that moment, Allal's old Peugeot drew up a few metres from the gate.

With a hesitant hand, Sarah lifted a corner of the curtain, as if lifting a taboo. Her heart was thumping so loudly, she was afraid it would waken the entire household.

Allal the policeman thought he saw a curtain twitch at a first-floor window. He could not make out Sarah's silhouette, but he knew she was there, as usual. He didn't linger. At Ghachimat, love was discreet, ripening slowly to avoid the evil eye. He furtively waved to her and drove off down the track.

Jelloul-the-fool was squatting under an olive tree, reviving a make-believe camp fire. On hearing the throbbing of the Peugeot, he straightened up and raised his hand to his temple. Even when the policeman drove past in the distance, Jelloul saluted him.

Sarah went back to bed and leaned against the pillow, her fingers crumpling the sheets as if to tear them.

Chapter four

Ammar the café-owner was setting up the tables on the pavement outside his establishment. A few puffy-eyed early morning customers were growing impatient on the other side of the street. They were waiting for the signal to rush for the domino sets. It was first come, first served, and latecomers would be disappointed. At Ghachimat, everybody fought for a seat in the café, attacking the day with thundering double-sixes and closing it with frustrating double-blanks. They remained glued to their seats until nightfall. From dawn till dusk, the joint echoed with the din of dominoes being slammed down, and by the time Ammar reached home, his head rang until he fell asleep.

Issa-the-disgrace was absorbed in a chore by the town hall. Holding a paper bag, he was picking up cigarette butts, paper and other refuse. Sitting on the steps, Maza the janitor watched him working flat out, and sniggered. From time to time, he hailed Issa, indicating a missed cigarette end with a jerk of his chin. Issa complied with disconcerting stoicism, pretending not to notice the janitor's glee.

"Try not to smoke them afterwards."

Issa contrived a smile and acquiesced.

"Don't stop, you shirker, there's more crap there, right under your nose."

The imam Salah walked past the town hall, looking disconsolate.

"Good morning, Sheikh," shouted the janitor.

"The only thing that's good is God," grumbled the imam. "When you come across a drunk who has found nowhere better to sleep it off than the mosque, first thing in the morning, you know the day bodes ill. Soon this village will be so infested with drunkards that our last patron saints will get the hell out of here."

The janitor threw up his arms in a gesture of dismay.

"And where are you off to, my good imam?"

"To hell, my son, to hell."

The imam left, the janitor stubbed out his cigarette on a step, flicked it onto the pavement and called Issa back to point it out to him.

Jafer Wahab's mother erupted when she found her son still in bed.

"You'll puff up like dough. Come on, up, I've got the housework to do."

Jafer stirred lazily beneath the covers.

"What time is it?"

"Since when did you care about the time? Your father and your brothers are working their fingers to the bone cleaning the well, and you don't give a hoot."

"My father will never get anything out of this damned land," grumbled Jafer drowsily. "I've told him. He doesn't want to know. Everybody knows there's no water in the well. He can dig as deep as he likes, he'll probably reach right to the bottom, but he won't find a single drop of water. If I were him, I'd sell the fields, buy myself a little business and live a life of leisure. We'd have a house instead of this kennel, and a car to drive around the countryside in, why not? It's so simple. Happiness is within everyone's grasp, you just have to reach out and grab your share. But my father is a wretch. He's suspicious of everything that doesn't make him suffer."

"If only your arm was as long as your tongue," replied his mother, with a heavy heart.

Jafer dropped in to see Kada the schoolteacher first, but he wasn't home. So he went back to the town square to watch the travelling souk setting up its makeshift stalls. Broken-down vans and carts cluttered the esplanade in an indescribable chaos. Housewives wandered from stall to stall, sniffing the fish, weighing the melons and shooing away the flies besieging the chunks of meat displayed on filthy slabs. A pot-bellied butcher whispered to the passers-by:

"It'll melt in your mouth. Suckling lamb, slaughtered this morning. No risks, my son's a vet."

Jafer was soon repelled by the stench. He wandered off towards the Sidhoms', in the absurd hope of meeting the policeman, mooned around, then listlessly ambled off into the fields. At the foot of the hill, he came across Mourad and his gang beside a bend in the river, smoking hashish. Mourad's eyes were already glazed. His brother, Boudjema, was avidly sucking a mangled cigarette, under the gaze of Lyès, the crafts-man in wrought iron. Zane-the-dwarf chuckled in his corner, rubbing his hands with a crab-like gesture. He had pulled the wings off a fly and deposited it in a hole in the sand. The distraught creature was trying to climb up the sides. The sand trickled away under its feet, and it slithered down. Suddenly, a little bump below the surface erupted, and an antlion snapped at the fly. As if by magic, the sand closed over the predator and its prey, leaving the dwarf jubilant.

"You look like a lost puppy," Lyès said to Jafer. "Has your friend the cop dropped you again?"

"That's life."

"Do you want a joint? I'll let you have it cheap. If you're skint, you can pay me later."

"At your own risk."

On the other side of the river, shrubs swayed at the sudden whim of a capricious wind, like supplicants. A field-mouse poked its tiny, pointed head up amid the stones. On the alert, it looked around a dozen times before venturing its whiskers in a puddle of water. The heat hung above the scorch-ing stones, making the atmosphere even more stifling and inducing lethargy. Jafer waited for the joint, which was not forthcoming. Bitterness clouded his face like a grey litham. Without knowing why, he told his friends:

"My father said to me: if you answer yes to all the following questions, I'll allow you to take the wife of your choice. Have you a job? I said no. Have you a private fortune?

I said no. Have you a roof? I said no. Then my father opened his arms and said: you'll just have to accept things, my son."

Lyès stared at him for a moment, rolled over onto his back and said wearily:

"You're going nuts, my friend."

"I think so too."

Zane-the-dwarf let out a strange cry, brandishing his fist like a trophy. His other hand immediately helped neutralize the fly, plucked it with a gleeful cackle and threw it into the antlion's nest. Jafer found it distressing. He stood up, saying:

"You make me sick."

Chapter five

"I won't go and grovel to that bitch. Besides, I have no intention of being associated with a family of pretentious upstarts."

Kada the schoolteacher's mother reeled, her mouth frothing with indignation. With each outburst, her heavy breasts rose, and her elephantine hips quivered. Her bloodshot eyes strafed the room.

"A filthy cow who acts as if she's married to the sultan because that scumbag of a husband of hers is the mayor. She soon forgot the days when she used to come to our farm to rummage in our dustbins. You should have seen her, barefoot with a runny nose, numb with cold, hardly daring to say thank you when I slipped a few coins into her hand. Then, suddenly, the heavens smiled on her, and now she's surrounded by admiring gossips. But when you go and see her,

she acts all high and mighty and says she's expecting people
. . . No, I won't go and grovel to her. I'd rather die."

Kada was sitting on the patio striped with shafts of light
filtering through the reeds. His mother's voice pounded his
temples like a flood.

"Enough!" he yelled, jumping to his feet.

The mother knew at once that her son was in the grip
of the devil.

"Listen," he said in a worrying voice. "We're no longer
living in the days when people used to choose a beast of
burden who would hold her tongue and be obedient to their
son. Nowadays, there's such a thing as love. And I *love* Sarah.
I don't give a damn about the mayor, his wife, your vanity
or gossip. What I want is Sarah. And you, Mother, despite
all the possible affronts imaginable, you're going to go over
there with your daughters and a tray of delicacies, and ask for
her hand, simply because I *want* it."

"It's out of the question."

"I'm afraid that *is* the whole question," he replied, his
voice growing hoarse and acrimonious. "I've made a lot of
concessions in my life. I agreed to become a rural schoolteacher
when I dreamed of being an aviator. I agreed to be *your* pup,
when I wanted to stand on my own two feet. Each time I
wanted to try my luck, you knelt down and begged me to
stay within reach of your selfishness. Now, I love a girl and
I want to marry her. Devil's daughter or king's daughter, she's
the girl I want, and that's it. And this time, I won't give in.
I'd rather die."

"What's she got that your cousins haven't? She's so thin
and pale, she looks as though she's dying."

"That's not what I think."

"She must have bewitched you. There's no doubt: she's put a spell on you. First thing tomorrow, I'll go and see an exorcist."

"You'll go and ask for her hand. There are many suitors after Sarah. Already Allal the cop is planning to marry her. And he's not the only one. We've got to act fast. If you try to put a spoke in my wheel, Mother dear, I'll ask Aunt Yasmina to represent me."

"Oh no! Not that viper. I couldn't bear it."

Mother and son glowered at each other for a long time, she flushed, he sullen. She had never suspected such fierce, such *suicidal* determination in him. She nodded, defeated.

"I don't recall having failed in my devotion," she sobbed, shaken up. "I can cope with having a bad sister, a bad husband is bearable, but your own son, your own little runt, that's appalling."

She collapsed on a seat like a shattered dream.

Kada did not sleep a wink all night. Sometimes lying on his bed, sometimes pacing up and down his room, he waited for morning. His many religious books failed to distract him. Each time he opened one, the pages became blurred, and it was Sarah's eyes that he saw. A feeling of disloyalty towards Allal the policeman gnawed away at his insides. He quickly refused to feel guilty and decided he had as much right as anyone else to aspire to the woman of his dreams.

At last dawn came. Kada performed his ablutions and

prayed at length. In the neighbouring room, his mother was protesting:

"That cow has to understand that the real honours are those you inherit, not the ones that come and go with promotion. I'm a Hilal, I am. In my day, I was called *Lalla*."

She spent an hour in front of her mirror, emphasizing each eyelash, each hair, camouflaging her disfiguring wrinkles and rolls of flesh under touches of make-up, cursing the unfortunate, green-tinged beauty spot tattooed on her cheek. Then, she spent ages choosing the most impressive ornaments from her jewellery collection.

Meanwhile, Kada paced up and down the veranda, his hands clasped behind his back. The Hilals' patio had seen moments of glory. Built by his great-grandfather, who had a mystical love of pomp and ostentation, it spread out below, ornamented with arches and flagstones. On the festival of Eid, they had entertained dozens of notables, and whole spit-roasted sheep had lined the entire length of the esplanade. The photos in the family albums, which his mother eagerly showed her friends, revealed endless orchards of apricot, cherry and almond trees in a carnival of blossom; the flunkeys decked out in tight-fitting embroidered waistcoats, glittering turbans and wide, baggy trousers. The grandfather like a *pasha* surrounded by his courtiers; the magnificent date palms marking the boundaries of the estate; the stable where, so legend had it, the most splendid pure-bred horses were reared. Nothing survived of this fairy-tale existence other than the ageing house, a section of the esplanade and a few scrawny trees. The rest had been confiscated under the Agrarian Reform and given over to the "common" people. In the former gardens, the new occupants had marked out plots of onions and grotesque flower beds that were criss-crossed by ditches permanently swarming with larvae and mosquitoes.

The mother finally appeared, her daughters in tow.

"Be on your best behaviour," said Kada.

"Why don't you come with us?" asked his mother. "You don't think you can teach us manners, do you? I'm a *caid*'s daughter. I'm not likely to forget myself in front of an old guttersnipe."

She brushed him aside disdainfully and went out, her head held high, a withering look in her eye.

"Have you got the book I recommended?" asked Tej Osmane, making himself comfortable in the wicker chair.

Kada was irritated by the mechanic's effrontery. Never had the latter dared cross the Hilals' threshold before. He preferred to wait for him humbly in the street. While Kada took his time, Tej would wait, in the sun or the rain, not even allowing himself to shelter under the entrance arch. Since the return of Sheikh Abbas, the son of Issa-the-disgrace had discreetly but determinedly been trying to put on a brave face. His tone became more confident each day, cautious, it was true, and sufficiently respectful to avoid rejection. His gestures became more expansive as a result of all the secret meetings, and his gaze, usually evasive, gradually learned to meet that of others with assurance. An accomplished hunter, he was always on the alert for the slightest chance to move up a rung. Sheikh Abbas treated him well. Already, a few brothers particularly "asked for" him. Tej never said no to anyone. It was his particular way of guaranteeing his rehabilitation. With each display of gratitude, no matter how covert, he regained a large part of his citizenship. The pernicious little insinuations here and there that needled him, the meaningful silences that marked his intrusions, and all the spiteful conniving that tormented him were becoming few and far between, and the fabric that held him hostage to his father's "crime" was beginning to fray, like an old rag. Tej Osmane was being "born". Absolutely. The day that finally saw his entry into the world would have a taste of ashes. That, in Ghachimat, people knew, and dreaded!

"You seem very preoccupied," he said to the school-teacher.

"I'm not too good."

Tej placed his foot on his knee, presenting the sole of his shoe to his host. Kada was offended. Tej knew it. As he maintained a surly silence, the mechanic ventured:

"It's because you shut yourself away, that's all. You hardly ever come and listen to the Sheikh. When I recommend a book, you don't show any interest in it."

"I'm going through a period of turmoil. I need to think about what's happening to me."

"You're right. If you want to move towards the holy truth, question yourself every time you doubt. What's the problem, exactly?"

"It's not really a problem."

"Do you want to talk about it?"

"It's personal."

Tej clearly sensed the rebuff and pretended to ignore it.

"That's precisely what friends are for."

Kada kept quiet. He sat there brooding in the hope that the mechanic would leave. Tej did not leave. He took a perverse pleasure in staying, gazing at the veranda and the vestiges of a reign now crippled.

"It's a beautiful house," he acknowledged. "But ostentation is so transient. When are you going to let your beard grow, Kada? The Sheikh insists. To identify ourselves. After all, it's a Sunna . . ."

"Please, Tej."

Tej raised his hands in apology. He went into the garden and crouched in front of the flowers. The schoolteacher seemed shocked to see the son of Issa taking an interest in nature, when normally he was covered in engine grease. He even felt a shudder of revulsion when the mechanic's hand grabbed a stem and snapped it.

"I've always dreamed of having a garden with masses of wallflowers, primulas, ivy on the walls and a few pomegranate trees."

Kada said nothing.

Tej's lips curled in a cynical grin. His eyes suddenly looked like burning embers.

"I've got to go," he said. "It's time to go and fetch the Sheikh."

He departed, leaving the door open behind him.

"Dragged through the mud by my own son," raged the mother coming onto the patio. "I should have smothered him between my thighs at birth."

35

Without a glance at her son, she swept across the court-yard and vanished into the house, her daughters at her heels.

The schoolteacher did not move a muscle. For three minutes, he sat there dumbfounded. Then his Adam's apple began to tremble and his hands, gripping his *kamis*, grew white at the knuckles. He controlled himself for a long time, fighting against the urge to destroy everything around him. Anger was unleashed inside him, screeching, chaotic.

Sarah would not be his.

From that day, he started growing a beard, and nobody could say whether it was to comply with Sheikh Abbas' recommendations or to mourn an old childhood dream.

Part 2

Chapter six

Dactylo was the public letter-writer at Ghachimat. Nobody knew where he had come from. One morning in '63, the village found him in the place he occupies today, just in front of the town hall, under a huge plane tree, sitting at a folding table, a ream of paper within reach of one hand, and a typewriter before him. At first, people looked for a maniacal glint in his eye. In those days the country was emerging from the war, its memory devastated, and there were lunatics every-where. But Dactylo seemed normal. His movements were coherent. There was just that strange frenzy that gripped him when he began to type on his keyboard, but onlookers found that more entertaining than disturbing. They thought he would soon gather up his miserable paraphernalia and vanish as suddenly as he has arrived. Dactylo stayed.

He liked the little place. Ghachimat reminded him of

his own people, quiet and lazy. The idea of becoming a big village did not even flicker across anyone's mind. These people had no intention of joining the rat-race and polluting Ghachimat. It was enough for the village simply to be there, at the end of a path or on the other side of a hillock, sitting squat amid its orchards, to believe itself the epicentre of the world. People here smiled readily, were open and warm, and, unlike city-dwellers, were unselfish.

Dactylo fell in love with the locality. As he didn't bother anyone, the village adopted him. His voice rarely carried beyond the contours of his lips. He was an easy-going man, always available, thoughtful and discreet, and, when he wasn't pounding away at his typewriter, he spent his time straining his eyes deciphering fat books full of "mumbo-jumbo" and staring at the tree tops.

It was Jelloul-the-fool who nicknamed him Dactylo. At first, customers flocked from all four corners of the region, bearing chickens, sugar loaves and baskets of eggs. When they began to bring him barren women, people who were possessed or epileptic, Dactylo found it impossible to explain that he was neither a marabout, nor an exorcist, but a public letter-writer, and that his job was to write letters and fill in forms for those who couldn't read or write. It took people a while to grasp, and then the endless queue began to dwindle and there was less and less of a clackety-clack by the town hall.

"Aren't you sick of your job?" asked Jafer Wahab, fiddling with his shoe laces.

Dactylo shrugged:

"It's my choice."

"That's what I mean."

"What do you mean?"

Jafer awkwardly pretended to fumble in his pockets. Dactylo guessed what he was up to. He had got to know everyone. He called a boy and asked him to go and fetch them two cups of coffee from Ammar's.

"How much do you earn at it?"

"I eat every day."

"I take my hat off to you, I really do. Sitting there, from dawn to dusk, typing and reading. I wouldn't be able to stay put for five minutes."

The boy returned with the coffee, walking with small steps, stopping each time the beverage slopped over into the saucers. Dactylo thanked him, slipped a coin into his hand and dismissed him. Jafer hurriedly lit a cigarette.

"I'm about to go mad," he said.

Dactylo took a sip and clicked his tongue with appreciation.

He said nothing. He knew that Jafer had come to get something off his chest, as he always did when things were too much for him – in other words, every day – and he was beginning to tire of playing the psychologist. Jafer was someone who was constantly dissatisfied, who had never really known what he wanted. Apart from indulging in alcohol and dope, he didn't know what else to do with his life.

On the other side of the river, Tej Osmane and his novices were hastening towards the Xaviers' farm, where Sheikh Abbas had elected to officiate. Every day, a growing group of new recruits left the village to go and worship the young imam. The meetings would go on late into the night.

"Beware of mixing with that mob down there," said Dactylo in a hollow voice.

"I'm not interested in that sort of thing," Jafer reassured him. "Besides, they're wasting their time. Nobody will go along with their ideas."

"You don't think? The country is as fragile as a hymen. It's just flashy slogans on the façades, a fanatical lie. Nothing but hot air. I know you don't notice much, but take a look at your village, prick up your ears and try to hear what the walls know, discover what lies beneath its deceptive lethargy, what is being hatched in obscure corners. Things are going on all the time, Jafer, like seeds escaping from a hole in a sack which, if you don't pick them up, will germinate. Hatred is burgeoning. Resentment is gaining the upper hand."

He suddenly broke off. His face clammed up. Jafer stared at him and then looked at Tej's group.

"They're just morons," he said without conviction.

Just then a taxi screeched to a halt in front of the café, covering the peasant farmers sitting at outdoor tables in dust. The ashen-faced driver clambered out and rushed inside. A few customers rose, intrigued, and crowded round the door, arousing the curiosity of the others. The taxi-driver had just come back from the city. He did not usually return until dark. Slumped over the counter, he drained two cups of coffee one after the other.

"Did you pick up the devil hitch-hiking?" asked Ammar.

It dawned on the taxi-driver that everyone was watching his lips. To heighten the suspense, he ordered a third coffee.

"No way. Out with it! Now!"

The taxi-driver mopped his face with a handkerchief, glancing surreptitiously between his fingers to gauge the attention he was receiving. Satisfied, he shouted:

"Alger's a bloodbath!"

"What? Have the Moroccans dared to attack us?"

"The people are rising up," explained the taxi-driver. "Thousands of youths have taken to the streets. Shops and office blocks have been burned down. The cops don't know which way to turn. They fired into the crowd. Dozens of people are said to have been killed. That's what they said on the radio, which is never wrong."

The news flared up like a haystack. Zane-the-dwarf was the first to react. He managed to squeeze between people's legs and ran shouting into the street:

"Alger's at war. Hundreds of dead. The people are rising up against the government."

"The whole of Alger's been burned down," added a peasant farmer. "Thousands are already dead."

An old man tore off his turban, flung it to the ground and stamped on it furiously:

"I told you *they*'d be back. De Gaulle is merciless."

"It's not the French. It's the people rising up against the bastards who've been keeping them down."

The old man froze, incredulous:

"What are you talking about? People are rising up against the *Raïs*? I'm going to get my gun now. I won't allow anyone to touch the President."

The village was in a ferment. People were running everywhere, calling each other and gesticulating. Women hurriedly gathered their children. The shock wave had spread from the café to the remotest alleys of the little town.

Hadji Maurice pushed back his hat to watch the confusion. He stopped Issa Osmane to ask him what was going on. Issa beat his hands as a sign of distress.

"The President's palace has been stormed by the demonstrators. They say he's about to abdicate."

"Apparently he's been wounded," added Zane jubilantly. "The army's occupying the capital, but neither the tanks nor the paras are able to control the uprising. Some people reckon there are as many as ten thousand dead."

The taxi-driver realized that he was alone amid the empty tables. He went back to his vehicle and drove off to notify the authorities. He found the mayor in his garden, talking business with Kouider Recham, a wealthy local entrepreneur.

"Have you heard the radio?"

The mayor darted the taxi-driver a reproachful look for disturbing him.

"Heard what?"

"Alger's burning."

"This isn't the fire station."

"I tell you, there's a mass uprising. There's shooting everywhere. The police are out of their depth. Dozens of people have been killed."

The mayor patted his guest's hands by way of apology for this irritating intrusion, rose and went to scrutinize the voluble firebrand who was so rude that he had not even bothered to introduce himself.

"My dear chap," he muttered with the false affability

that belies controlled anger, "the country is on edge. The protest demonstrations are simply biological. A few years ago in Oran we saw a similar hysteria. They were forgiven, because it's only natural. You for example, I expect you break the odd plate over your wife's head. But once your anger's abated, you forget all about it. Don't overdramatize the situation, my friend, don't overdramatize. Our people tend to make a lot of noise, but their bark is worse than their bite. When they get carried away, it doesn't mean much. It's all hot air, do you understand? It's good to let off steam from time to time. It's healthy. Just you wait, tomorrow everything will be back to normal."

He shoved the taxi-driver outside.

"By the way, have you paid your arrears?"

The taxi-driver gulped anxiously.

"Not yet, sir."

"You see? Suppose you concentrate on paying your over-due taxes instead of listening to subversive radio stations?"

The taxi-driver hung his head, embarrassed:

"You are absolutely right, sir."

"Are you an official like me?"

"No, sir."

"Are your concerns national, as mine are?"

"No, sir."

"So leave the nation's officials to manage the nation's problems."

"I don't know what got into me, sir."

The taxi-driver climbed back into his car and roared off without a backward glance.

"Stupid idiot," cursed the mayor, slamming the iron gate.

Chapter seven

The silence was shattered by Jelloul-the-fool's long, pathetic laugh, half yelp and half lugubrious wail. The women had got into the habit of spitting on their breasts to ward off evil when it rang out like that, at the hour when the night hitches up her skirts to reveal the purulent wounds of sunrise. When Jelloul's manic laugh echoed at daybreak, the dawn chorus fell silent, and the dogs cowered in their corner, their tails tucked under their bellies and their eyes apprehensive. People on their way home from the mosque stopped in their tracks, puzzled, a finger on their chin, wondering from which direction despair would howl.

That morning, it burst forth from the Kerroum's house: Sidi Saim had not risen at the muezzin's call. His niece had found him stretched out on his mat, face down. Death had taken advantage of his sleep to abduct him from his family.

Sidi Saim was the village elder. He was the source of wisdom and moral authority. Although not the tribes' soul, he was their memory. Each wrinkle on his forehead was a verse, each hair of his beard a prophecy. How many frenzied rages had been soothed by his gaze, how many arguments dissipated at the sound of his voice. He had been a revered sheikh during the time of French rule, a living marabout afterwards, and it was absolutely "legitimate" for the Elders to decide, unanimously, to build a mausoleum in his memory.

"It's a heresy!" stated Abbas, peremptorily.

Gathered in the mosque, the Elders exchanged outraged looks. The imam looked up at the young sheikh standing in the doorway and said:

"My son . . ."

"I am not your son . . . It's time to put an end to these pagan traditions. Sy Saim is dead. We can't bring him back to life. All we can do is consign him to the earth, quietly and without a fuss. Like all common mortals, he will be entitled to a simple grave, without a tombstone or epitaph, and to a prayer. Any other improvisations would be sinful."

His fervent gaze settled on the deceased man's son, a shy, sickly man in his fifties. He went on:

"How can you allow them to place your father among the corrupt? He remained poor and humble, despite his erudition. What is happening to you, Muslims of Ghachimat? Hamza himself lies in a simple grave, naked in the naked earth, to remind the vain of their weakness . . . The body, once it becomes lifeless, is nothing but a vulgar tissue of lies. Worms would not eat it away if it deserved any consideration in the eyes of the Lord."

The notables attempted to protest. In the street, Abbas' followers wore belligerent expressions. Since October 1988, which had seen Alger rise up against the monsters of the régime, the Muslim Brothers had been inexorably emerging from clandestinity. Each day, the tribal hierarchy that controlled the destiny of the *douar*, which conferred birthright on some and demanded filial respect from all, saw itself being edged out by the young protesters. The Elders tried to regain a grip, but their endless shilly-shallying allowed the Sheikh's rapacious and dangerously expansionist flock to gain ground.

Hadji Maurice was the first to set off for the cemetery, because of his obesity. He had to stop to catch his breath every hundred metres.

"You should have used a cart," admonished Hadji Menouar.

"Bah, it's good to get a bit of exercise."

"Yes, but at this rate we're likely to miss the address."

"We're an hour early."

Hadji Menouar caught sight of the funeral procession leaving the village.

"They're coming . . ."

Hadji Maurice made a gesture of exhaustion. His shirt was steaming in the blazing heat. He leaned on his stick but was unable to get to his feet again. Hadji Menouar placed his hand under his armpit and helped heave him up, revealing a huge damp patch on the rock where they had been sitting.

"Doing that to Sidi Saim," lamented Hadji Menouar. "It's an outrage."

"You know, the pyramids haven't brought the mummies back to life."

"They protect them against oblivion."

"But not against men, in any case."

The procession caught up with them about a hundred metres from the cemetery. The Elders led the way, without real solemnity. They had given in to Abbas and trailed their surrender like a shameful disease.

The crowd spread out around the grave that Issa Osmane was digging. They allowed him to finish off, then someone snatched the shovel and the fork. The imam stumbled through the funeral address. His grief and indignation rebelled against his words and, despite his efforts to hold them back, tears formed on his eyelashes like a howl of rage.

The patron saints had fallen from grace. They succumbed to the storm of affronts as trees lose their foliage at the onset of autumn.

That evening, in the café, the domino players sat with their heads in their hands. The narrow streets were silent. The wind, muffled by the dust, whirled like a jinnee in a trance. Tej Osmane and his fundamentalist cronies were strutting around the square. The more attention their parade attracted, the higher they raised their chins. Their guru had reduced the Elders to the rank of subordinates. They were aware of the significance of such a concession and they were not planning to stop there.

Perched on a wall, Zane-the-dwarf looked like a night owl. His dilated pupils shone with a terrifying fire. He *knew* that his revenge was at hand, that time was already on his side.

"Patience has its limits," remarked Hadji Ali.

The imam watched a moth flying giddily around the lamp adorning the pediment of Hadji Maurice's house. Thousands of stars twinkled in the blue-tinged sky. It was night, and Ghachimat was unable to sleep.

The Elders sat brooding on the balmy patio. The tea had gone cold, and nobody had touched their glass. From time to time, a voice rose up and was immediately transformed into a long sigh.

"I wonder whether it mightn't be wise to withdraw our children from the school," said Hadji Baroudi. "Those teachers cram their heads with nonsense and turn them against us."

"You're right," said Hadji Bilal. "My kid isn't even ten and he's already making offensive remarks."

"Mine have literally threatened me," said Dahou the shopkeeper. "At four o'clock in the morning, they're up like prison guards, and they kick their sisters awake for morning prayer. And woe betide anyone who protests. I've tried to intervene. My eldest pushed me away. Not for a second was he ashamed of raising his hand to his father."

"*Astaghfiru 'llah,*" replied the imam indignantly. "On the Last Day it is said that the bowels of the earth will spew forth flames higher than the mountains, and that everywhere, howling gnomes will emerge from the abysses, invade the land and decimate mankind faster than a devastating epidemic."

"Could we have unwittingly become infidels?" cried Hadji Ali.

Someone knocked at the door. The Elders looked about fearfully.

"Are you expecting anyone?"

"Not really," said Hadji Maurice sleepily.

Dahou the shopkeeper went to open the door. Hadji Boudali entered mumbling, his expression aghast.

"Oh, you're here. Thank God . . ."

"Sit down. You look . . ."

"I didn't come here to spin yarn," ranted Hadji Boudali. "This situation has gone on too long. We've got to do something, now. I've left my bastard of a son for dead. I didn't bring a brat into the world to be ruled by him."

The old men noticed the bloodstains on Hadji Boudali's *gandoura*. His bludgeon was broken. A large graze on his wrist was bleeding.

"I hope you haven't killed him . . ."

"I should care. Calling me a turncoat, me, his father, three times a pilgrim. Never once did I allow myself to look up at my father. I didn't even dare approach my children in his presence. I kissed his hand every time I met him. He was ungrateful, bad-tempered, unpredictable and suspicious, and not once did I forget that he was first and foremost my father. Today, my offspring treat me as if I were Iblis himself, after I've half starved myself to death to feed and educate them . . ."

He pushed away Dahou who tried to calm him and went back into the street shouting: "I'm going home to finish him off, the bastard. Tonight he'll lie in hell."

The old men ran after the agitated father. Left alone, Hadji Maurice settled down in his corner, placed his hands on his stomach and prepared to go to sleep.

"I heard shouts," said Tej Osmane appearing in the doorway.

"It's nothing. Go home."

Tej nodded obligingly. Before leaving, he contemplated the patio bathed in light and the carefully maintained garden, and there was a strange glint in his eyes.

Chapter eight

The Xaviers' farm had become a real pilgrimage centre. The big stable, converted to a prayer hall, was full to bursting point. Latecomers had to sit on the ground in the farmyard, virulent sermons ringing in their ears. A tannoy, suspended from the top of the building, trumpeted the speakers' diatribes across the countryside, summoning passers-by for miles around.

Mourad took advantage of a pause to signal his followers to follow him out on tiptoe, pretending not to notice the disapproving look of Tej Osmane, who was becoming increasingly bold. Once on the other side of the hill, away from indiscreet ears, Mourad grabbed Zane by the neck as if to wring it:

"Is *that* your surprise? You've made me waste a day to listen to idiotic ranting."

Zane tried to struggle free.

"I thought you'd be interested . . ."

"I don't give a damn about that rabble. Can you see me with a banner and a sabre, persecuting poor wretches?"

He pushed away the dwarf who bent double, coughing exaggeratedly.

Boudjema was overawed. His face was unimaginably radiant. He said:

"Abbas is a genius."

"Who are you to tell the difference between a genius and a trickster?" groaned Lyès-the-craftsman. "Abbas is off his head if you want my opinion. He's a utopian, that's all. I just want to be left to booze in peace. I don't bother anyone, and I don't want anyone to pester me."

A car drew level with them and stopped. Jafer Wahab leaned out, his jaw hanging open and his face concealed behind huge sunglasses. He jerked his thumb at Allal Sidhom sitting behind the wheel.

"My driver's back. This evening we're going to see the whores and have ourselves a ball."

"Lucky you," retorted Lyès without enthusiasm.

"Hey, our cop's getting married in two months' time. You're all invited to the wedding."

"We know."

Jafer waved at the group and leaned back in his seat, pedalling in the void, as happy as a kid. The car moved off, bouncing over the ruts. A swarm of women arrived from the village, closely guarded by a man astride a donkey. His legs were so long that they scraped the dust. Allal had to mount the embankment to let them pass. Further on, he overtook

Issa Osmane hobbling towards the village, a fifty-kilo bag of flour on his shoulders.

"You'll end up with a hernia," remarked Jafer. "Throw your bundle into the boot and get in the back."

Issa wobbled under the weight of his burden. Without stopping, he said:

"The sinner must redeem himself by his toil alone, my boy. Thank you all the same."

And he hurried out of the way.

The mayor was standing in front of his residence. He signalled to Allal to pull over to the side. The policeman was so embarrassed that he nearly hit a boulder.

"We've been waiting for you, dear boy," said the mayor, enveloping him in an embrace. "So how was your assignment in Alger?"

"It looks as if things are settling down."

"Let's hope so. The country's got enough problems as it is." Taking him by the elbow and steering him away from Jafer, he went on: "I saw the builders at your place. If you need money, don't hesitate to ask. Your father and I were great friends. Besides, now we're one family."

"I am honoured, sir."

"Good."

Allal went back to the car and got into a muddle with the gearstick. Beside him, Jafer laughed up his sleeve, feeling both amused and sorry for him.

"Your future father-in-law gives you the jitters."

"Shut up, he might hear you."

"Your ears are as red as tomatoes."

The mayor walked off. Before starting up the engine,

Allal looked up at the garden where Sarah was pretending to water the flowers, taking care not to look over towards the road.

"Ah," exclaimed Jafer, "if only I were a cop."

"I thought you wanted to be a lion?"

"Unfortunately lionesses don't have manes."

"Watch it," burst out Allal, "that's my fiancée you're talking about."

At the end of his leave, Allal realized that Kada had not wanted to see him even once. Hilal's son would not leave Sheikh Abbas' side for a moment. When he went home, he refused to entertain his friends. Allal also noticed that the streets infested with brats and dogs, the abandoned fields, and the air itself were heavy with resentment. There was only one name on people's lips: Abbas . . . Abbas said . . . Abbas thinks . . . Abbas has decided . . . The Elders had lost face. Their status had plummeted almost as low as that of Issa Osmane; they hugged the walls, their turbans weighing down oppressively. Hadji Boudali had publicly repudiated his son. He had implied that his next pilgrimage would be one-way, that he would gladly die at Minen or Ghar Hira. Something had snapped inside his head. Every evening, he went and stoned the evil spirits that haunted the *oued*. He swore he saw them clearly among the dancing shadows of the oleanders. The imam, too, had surrendered. His new audience, made up of youths and young men with bushy beards, shaved heads and eyes rimmed with khol, wanted no more of his preaching. They called him a fortune-teller, a parrot of the régime. When

two Brothers barred his entrance to the mosque, Dactylo said
to Jafer:

"The hideous beast is stirring."

And Jafer replied nonchalantly:

"They can go to the devil!"

"The devil is here."

Chapter nine

Sheikh Redouane sat enthroned on the *minbar* in his shimmering *jellabah*. He was handsome, tall and majestic. His right hand rested on his knee, like a sceptre. His holy travels throughout Muslim territories and his long spells in prison were legendary. He had been to Egypt, Pakistan and Malaysia, and everywhere the ground he trod became downy with a blessed grass. In the mosque, the Brothers felt purified merely by his presence. Some even went so far as to collect, in jars, the lustral water that had served for his ablutions. Those who had been near him swore his scent had the fragrance of Paradise. Many had fought hard to touch him with their fingertips; many had experienced ecstasy when his gaze fell on them.

To the right of the *minbar*, sitting on cushions facing the audience, Sheikh Abbas, Kada Hilal, Tej Osmane and three companions of the "enlightened traveller" were meditating.

Sheikh Redouane slowly raised his arm, as if to raise a suspect curtain. The audience held its breath. The higher his arm rose, the greater the sense of deliverance experienced by the gathering, like a levitation.

The speaker's voice boomed out.

"I saw a tomb on a hill, firmly planted on its feet, throwing not only its curse but also its vile shadow over a listless nation."

His voice flooded the mosque like a torrent in spate.

"I said: 'Who is this Houbel risen from the shadows?' *They* looked at me with scorn and replied: 'It is the mausoleum of the Martyr.' I said: 'There are cemeteries for the dead.' *They* cried in horror: 'Glory has its monuments too. Our children have a duty to drink at the fount of their history.' I said: 'So where is this glory, in Riad el-Feth? In those unlawful shops where underwear is exhibited like trophies? In those bars where people get drunk without shame? In those dark cinemas where people are taught smug voyeurism? ... So where is the martyr among those wretches?' No, my brothers, there has never been any place for the dead, even less for the destitute like you, in Riad-the-corrupt ... It is governed solely by the greed of the traitors and speculators, turning the people into a nation of layabouts and abandoning them ..."

A wave of indignation swept over the assembly.

"I lifted my gaze beyond the hill and I saw a bilious horizon, a threatening sky. And I understood why our country was ravaged by drought, why the earth had trembled at El-Asnam, and why it continued to tremble beneath our feet today . . . I said: 'People of Algeria, what are you doing under the debris? Why have you lowered your guard?' Nobody heard me. And I saw the spread of nepotism and vanity, abuse and coarseness, and I saw the crowd wandering blithely towards the torrents of vice. My people have lost their soul, lost their bearings, lost their hope. Its head has become the rubbish dump of the West. Heresy is nurtured there in the guise of transcendence. Our intellectuals prostitute themselves to pernicious cultures, our rulers indulge in all sorts of plunder, our women strip off in the name of emancipation, and we grope around in broad daylight, dazzled by the flames of hell."

"*Astaghfiru 'llah!*" wailed someone at the back of the room.

"With an aching heart, I rushed down the hill in the hope of meeting men of probity, far from this tainted place. And I saw the prophecy fleeing and disillusioned, in tatters, wretched and distraught, reviled, repudiated, discarded. And Sodom seemed nothing compared with Alger! . . ."

"*Allah O Akbar!*" cried a voice, to explosive effect.

"And when we say to them: 'O people, what you are doing is evil', they look at us with scorn, call our indignation 'extremism', our pain 'intolerance', our brave words 'sedition', and *they* call *us* the enemy. And when we offer them the book of the Lord, they brandish Marx, Sartre and Dante, reinforcing in front of us the walls of their DEMONcracy, and setting ruthless executioners against us. But we are unable to remain silent when God has been insulted. And we tell them, once and for all, without fear, woe to the infidels, woe to the infidels, woe to the infidels!"

Suddenly, the beards bristled, fists clenched and chests exploded:

"Cursed be the fiends, cursed be their dead and their living! . . ."

On the other side of Ghachimat were some ancient ruins that had attracted several generations of archaeologists. They had found utensils and flint weapons, and had long puzzled over the age-old signs etched onto the stones. When they had come to erect tents on the site and clear the rubble, the village children clustered on the surrounding hilltops and watched the archaeologists at work for hours on end. They didn't understand what all the fuss was about, but the energy of these magicians from the city was more than enough to liven up a deadly boring hillside.

Then one day, an order came down, like a blade, arbitrary and obtuse: the camp was packed up and the enclosure turned over to drunks and curious loafers once more. If it had not been for Sidi Saim's intervention, the temple would have vanished beneath a refuse tip by now. To preserve the site, and History, somebody had put it about that the place was haunted, and that at full moon, ghosts could be heard staggering around, their chains clanking, while from the bowels of the earth sepulchral voices rent the silence, piercing the mind like a rapier.

Dactylo was fond of the ruins. They afforded a splendid view over the valley, and the tranquillity and age of the place gave it a magical quality. Here, the sounds of the forest and the clamour of the village were muted, as if filters absorbed the dissonances. After hours of work, Dactylo would go there to relax and marvel at the very simple, delightful things that were part of the secret life of the night. But for some time his solitude had been marred by the irritating presence of Jafer Wahab who, drunk and maudlin, would not stop complaining about the arrogance of the silence and the pallor of the stars which boded ill.

Suddenly, from the village, they heard the cries of the Brothers. Dactylo turned his head towards the mosque.

"Sheikh Redouane is as inflammatory as a pyromaniac," he sighed.

Jafer kicked the wine bottle he had just drained and watched it roll into the ditch.

"He's the sixth sheikh to turn up here in less than two months. The mayor ought to ban the abuse of the tannoy," he muttered. "We can't hear ourselves any more, and their din has frightened away the birds."

Dactylo stood up:

"The wolves are about, the lamb had better return to the fold."

"Are you leaving me here all by myself?"

"Go home."

"My father's angry with me. Could I stay with you tonight? Allal's late back and I don't know what to do."

Dactylo looked peeved, his hands on his hips.

"I promise not to annoy you with my stupid questions. Please don't leave me alone. I don't feel good."

Dactylo thought, then signalled to him to follow.

The public letter-writer's house was hidden behind a row of carob trees. It wasn't quite part of the village, nor was it quite in the fields. It was as though it had opted for a happy medium. The interior was tidy, clean and airy, divided in half by a curtain; on one side was the kitchen, on the other the bedroom. Shelves laden with books filled half the room. On the walls painted off-white, some very old-looking black and white photos were displayed in wrought frames.

"Is that your family?"

Dactylo laughed silently.

"You could say that . . . that's Ahmad Shawqi on the right."

"Who's he? He looks important."

"An Egyptian poet, perhaps the greatest ever. This young man is Aboulkassem ech-Chabbi. He died very young, of tuberculosis."

"Who's the soldier?"

"Guillaume Apollinaire."

"Did he fight against us in the war?"

"Poets don't fight. They're sacrificed for noble causes, a bit like Christ. On the left that's Aleksandr Ostrovsky. There's Thomas Mann, and the other is Mohammed Dib."

"The one from the TV series?"

"I haven't got a TV."

"Are they all Muslims?"

"Those fellows are geniuses. Each nation wants to claim them, but they belong to the whole world. They are the human conscience, the only Truth."

Jafer turned round to look at the books. He caressed some of the bindings, carefully, as if they were holy relics.

"Have you read all these books?"

"Most of them."

"How come you don't wear glasses?"

Dactylo removed his jacket, rolled up the sleeves of his sweater and went into the kitchen.

"There are some magazines under the typewriter. Dinner will be ready in about half an hour."

"Do you clean the place yourself?"

"I can't afford a servant."

"You should take a wife."

Dactylo parted the curtain, showing his face:

"You promised . . ."

Jafer raised his hands in apology. After a brief silence, he charged in again:

"I hope it's not a genital problem."

"You certainly don't beat about the bush," laughed Dactylo.

Shouts erupted outside, followed by a string of obscenities and howls. The two men rushed out and found a group of youths armed with coshes beating Moussa, a solitary eccentric, calling him a drunkard who deserved to be burned at the stake.

"Hey, what are you doing?"

The thugs scattered, crowing triumphantly, leaving the tramp on the ground, his head covered in blood and his shirt in tatters. Dactylo ran to help him up. Moussa angrily pushed him away and, raising himself on all fours, he began to grope around in the dust.

"Bastards! What have they done with my bottle? I haven't even opened it."

"Come," invited Jafer, "don't stay there. They've made a mess of you, I'm going to take you to the medical centre."

The drunkard suddenly froze, stared the two men up and down and blurted out:

"I don't need anyone! I lick my own wounds, like a big boy."

With a final burst of pride, he stood up, adjusted his shirt with a shaking hand and walked away, dragging his leg with dignity.

Chapter ten

Another dismal day, sighed Jafer Wahab, strolling through the narrow streets.

With his shaggy beard and heavy eyebrows, 'Smail Ich was sitting on a crate watching his cubs painting the initials of the Islamic Salvation Front on the façade of the school. Each brush stroke gave him a thrill of satisfaction. From time to time he removed the liquorice stick from between his teeth to aim a gob of spittle as far as he could. When a passer-by paused in front of the graffiti, if he was a sympathizer, Jafer would ask him what he thought, and if he was a detractor, he would ask him to get out of the way. Content in both instances, he would flick his jaunty fez and go back to cleaning his teeth. When they had finished the school walls, he would go and draw his ornate letters on the walls of all the houses. Earlier, Dahou the storekeeper had tried to protest on seeing him scrawl *Vote FIS* on his shop front. 'Smail had replied: "We will write the name of the Lord where we see fit, and we will even copy His verses in your trade register."

Lurking under an arched doorway, Zane-the-dwarf was offering a gold chain to Messaoud, an occasional fence. The old man turned the necklace over in his expert hands and bit it to ascertain its authenticity.

"It's not fake, I assure you."

"Shut up, I know what I'm doing, and I don't like being rushed."

Zane smarmily complied.

"You're sure you got it in town?"

"There's no risk, I promise," swore Zane. "Its owner would never set foot around here."

Messaoud finally looked up, his lip drooping almost to his chin. The dwarf's imploring expression made him wary. He waited until a mule driver had gone past, affecting indifference.

"I don't want it."

"But business is good at the moment."

"That's because I don't play with fire. I've got enough trouble with my neighbours. I don't want any with the police."

Zane looked around him, at a loss. Old Messaoud remained impassive.

"Five hundred thousand, OK?"

"I tell you, I don't want it. It's too risky. If ever its owner found it at my place, I'd end my days in gaol. With my rheumatism, I wouldn't last a week. No, honestly," he added artfully, "it's not worth it."

"Four hundred? . . . Tell me your price, this is a democracy, isn't it? Prices are negotiable. Three hundred and fifty. I can't go any lower. This necklace is worth double that."

The fence took back the chain, deliberately checking each link, brooding indecisively, to aggravate the dwarf even more.

Further away, Hadji Maurice was inviting Jafer to have a glass of tea. Jafer crouched at the low table and wearily served himself.

"You don't look yourself, misery guts."

"Allal's the misery guts. I'm more happy-go-lucky."

"It's true," recalled the former schoolteacher. "He was always sickly, and you a fraud, but you were both equally naughty."

"But he's made up for it since."

"And what about you?"

"I'm waiting for the next train."

Hadji Maurice sensed his former pupil's lassitude and continued mopping himself with his handkerchief. Jafer was unhappy. He went round and round in circles, from dawn till dusk. Sometimes he would talk to himself and, each time he went past Hadji Maurice's house, the old man grew a little more concerned.

"When I think of your crazy essays . . ."

"That was Kada Hilal. He's the village schoolteacher now," said Jafer bitterly.

"That's life."

Jafer drank his tea and left, forgetting to thank the old man. On the street corner, he found himself face to face with Kada. The Brother glanced at the hem of his robe and grumbled:

"Mind where you step, you nearly ruined my *kamis*."

Jafer stared at the religious books his one-time friend was carrying. He found him very different with his aggressive beard and reptilian eyes.

"Why do you talk to me like that, Kada? What have I done to you? What exactly have you got against me? I can understand your avoiding me, but I can't understand for the life of me why you are so bitterly angry. Only a few weeks ago we were as inseparable as the fingers on a hand. And suddenly, without warning, you have only hatred and contempt for me. What has happened to you, son of the Hilals? Why do you detest me?"

"Detest you?" sneered Kada. "I've got better things to do, believe me. As far as I'm concerned, you barely exist."

"I'm not your enemy."

"Giants don't have enemies among the goblins."

He pushed him aside with disdain and carried on towards the mosque.

Belkacem was standing in front of his bakery, chatting to Tayeb the carter. Issa Osmane emerged from the bake house, covered in flour from head to foot, unloaded a sack, put it on his back and went back into the bakery. He came back for another. As he stooped under the weight of the load, the sack slid from his shoulders and burst open on the ground.

"Good-for-nothing!" shouted the baker. "What do you think you're doing?"

Embarrassed and terrified, Issa knelt down and began scooping up the flour in both hands to put it back in the sack.

"That's right, idiot. You'll get grit in the flour and my customers will break their teeth."

"I'll sort it out," promised Issa in a tremulous voice.

"I'm the one who'll sort you out, you stupid ass. I'm sure you did it on purpose and you're going to pay for it."

"How much does he owe you?" a voice rang out behind them.

Tej Osmane was at the corner of the street. He was mad with rage, but he remained calm. He walked towards his father, grabbed him by the collar of his jacket and ordered him to get up. Belkacem tried to intervene, Tej pushed him away and advised him not to get involved.

"It's between your father and me," insisted the baker. "That stupid . . ."

"Another word and I'll punch your face in."

Belkacem could not believe his ears. Issa-the-disgrace's son had never dared raise his eyes, let alone his voice, in front of the people of Ghachimat. He tore off his jacket. The onlookers knew that the clash was inevitable. Delighted to be the privileged witnesses, they gathered around the bakery, affecting indignation, urging the two men not to content themselves with insults, like women.

"How much does he owe you?" said Tej, not particularly enthusiastic about the brawl.

"All your teeth, son of a bitch!"

Belkacem's fist flew out at once. He was powerful but over-confident. Tej ducked and reacted with rare violence. Caught off-guard, the baker was knocked out after a few blows, his face covered in blood. Jafer hurled him to the ground and continued pummelling him.

"That's enough!" yelled his father. "You'll kill him . . ."

Tej calmed down, wiped his arm across his sweaty brow, extricated a few bank notes from his pocket and flung them nonchalantly onto the body lying on the ground.

"From today," he proclaimed to all around him, "my father and I have no more creditors."

Back home, Tej grabbed his father by the shoulders and said:

"It's finished, do you hear?"

"What's finished, son?"

"The humiliation. From now on, you're going to hold your head up high and walk upright among men. Nobody will dare look you in the eye, I promise. I'm going to shut them up once and for all."

Issa shook his head sadly:

"Where's that going to get us, my son? They're all no-hopers. I've seen them begging, not for bread, or money, but just for a little compassion. They were masters at toadying to the *caid* and licking his boots. In calling me names today, all they're doing is betraying themselves, one by one. Let them spit at me when I go past, it won't cleanse them of the filth they ate in the days when they grovelled and called me 'sidi'. Independence didn't rehabilitate them. It just allowed them to forget themselves, to forget their baseness and their insignificance, to revenge themselves on scapegoats. They are incapable of forgiving, even less of making allowances."

A few weeks later, Issa Osmane was invited to a circumcision. Thinking it was a joke, he declined the invitation. Then, one day, a rich cattle merchant came to fetch him in person. And the factotum realized with amazement that the powerful car gleaming outside his shack was indeed there to fetch him. Soon, to his cost, Issa would discover that he was going to miss the people who exploited him after work hours, the little extra duties, the impossible errands asked of him at all hours of day and night, all those thankless little tasks that helped him make ends meet, and that his world and his larder would be the poorer. People had become respectful towards him, listening to his words. Overnight, his life was turned upside down. Each time Issa offered his services, in the hope of gleaning a few coins, people replied: "Come, come, Sy Issa. You can't do that." And Issa, both ironic and disappointed, would strike his forehead with his hand crying: "It's true, I'm emancipated now."

He had never thought himself capable of cynicism, nor had he suspected fundamental values of being so fluid. When he walked in the streets and saw his torturers of old fussing around him as though nothing had happened, or heard them laugh heartily at whatever nonsense he spoke, Issa was suddenly frightened at what was happening to him and sometimes regretted not having remained a victim, for never had he experienced true shame before being elevated to the rank of the notables.

Chapter eleven

"Beware of the curse of impotence," insisted Ghalia. "Avoid picking up any keys or suspicious-looking knives, if you don't want your kid's virility to let him down just when his honour depends on it."

Sidhom Allal's terrified mother assented, mindful of her sister's instructions.

They entered the bridal chamber and burned incense in the nooks and crannies, muttering incantations. Ghalia placed the smoking earthenware dish on the floor, took out a charm from her bosom and whirled it seven times above her head before placing it under the mattress:

"Oh Sidi Yacub, may our daughter-in-law be as loving as a she-cat, as fertile as a rabbit and as faithful as a bitch."

The women began to flock to the Sidhoms' house. Their ululating reflected their degree of enthusiasm – some wailed heartily, others feebly. The tambourines started up as soon as the musicians were settled, making the children cry. Hips were swathed in scarves and began to sway in a furious dance, not one bit intimidated by the scandalized gaze of the girls wearing *hijabs*.

Allal and his friends were staying with Lyès-the-craftsman at Moulay Naim, a neighbouring village. Lying curled up on the patio, Zane-the-dwarf was drifting peacefully into an alcoholic stupor. He had drunk from all the glasses and smoked from every pipe. Tej Osmane, who had proclaimed himself *vizir*, in other words, advisor to the groom, took his temporary role very seriously and with great obsequiousness was going from one guest to the next enquiring after their comfort.

Allal consulted his watch anxiously:

"They're late."

"It's probably because of the heat," Tej reassured him. "Maybe they decided to wait until it cooled down a little."

Allal was not relaxed. He sat down again and wiped his clammy hands on a handkerchief.

"Kada's also keeping us waiting," he commented disapprovingly. "You're not going to tell me it's because of the heat."

"You just concentrate on your wedding," advised Jafer, almost unconscious. "Everybody's been invited to your wedding. If there are some who are so jealous as to ignore you, it's not your problem. Here," he added, offering him a brownish paste, "try this. It's an aphrodisiac powerful enough to bust a lock."

'Smail Ich pushed open the garden gate and nearly trod on Zane, who was lying inert across the path.

"What's this shit!" he exclaimed before placing a bulky present in front of Allal.

Without asking for permission to open it, he sliced the ribbon with a stroke of his penknife, ripped off the wrapping paper and said:

"Sheikh Abbas sent you, didn't he?"

It was a few lines of calligraphy in gilt on black velvet, framed.

"*Ayat-ul-kursi,*" explained 'Smail. "This verse will protect you from bad influences."

"Please thank Abbas for me."

"Yes, yes, of course, officer. A fat lot of good that'll do him. Excuse me if I don't stick around with your friends. There are too many unhealthy influences around here."

Ghachimat had lit its street lamps earlier than usual. The mayor felt that he could allow himself certain whims. It wasn't every day that he married off his daughter. On the scrawny hillside, dusk was pursuing the last patches of daylight to the mountain top. In the coolness of evening, the impassioned beating of the tambourines rose up and dissipated over the fields.

Allal Sidhom put on his wedding suit and joined his friends on the patio. Zane unwisely emerged from his stupor. Tej solemnly announced that it was time to honour the virgin. He clapped his hands to request the guests to go out into the street where a white pure-bred was snorting impatiently. Allal was helped up into the saddle. At once, the procession set off amid a rowdy chorus and gunshots fired from old guns with wide muzzles.

Sarah was sitting on the marriage bed, her tiny hands trembling on her knees. The poet would be incapable of saying whether it was the lampshade on the bedside table or her, a summer-golden houri, which gave the room its fairytale atmosphere. Allal knelt before her and took her hand. His lips brushed the henna-stained fingers so clumsily that they failed to kiss them. He raised her veil, slowly, for fear of seeing the virgin's beautiful face vanish like an elusive dream. Sarah's eyes widened, as vast as a meadow. And that look alone, with its sublime reflections, was enough to make Allal forget the crowd outside clamouring noisily for the petticoat of truth.

Kada Hilal sat in his house, plunged in darkness, listening for the approach of the processions like a condemned man awaiting execution. His mother and sisters had gone into town so as not to attend the celebrations. He had stayed glued to the window, damning the whole village. He had eaten nothing all day. When Tej Osmane came to fetch him, he pretended not to be there. Once Tej had left, the schoolteacher rampaged through the garden, then he went into his room and hurled everything to the floor. On catching sight of the first convoy – Sarah's – he cursed her. Now it was Allal's turn to appear on his white horse. He rode past Kada, just within reach of his grief, handsome and radiant, his pack of merry entertainers swarming round him. Kada's legs buckled under him and he wanted to die before reaching the ground.

Part 3

Chapter twelve

It was a dishevelled, filthy and exhausted Kada Hilal who turned up, one pale morning, at the Xaviers' farm. His beard dangled from his chin like a spider's web. His gaping shirt was covered with large stains of dried vomit, and his shoes, battered by his wanderings, gaped like frogs' mouths. He dragged himself along, gripping a wall or a shoulder for support, stopping from time to time to blow his nose or to turn round, in search of who knows what. In the farmyard resembling a parade ground, the Brothers stared at him in disbelief and looked away when his gaze fell wretchedly at their feet.

'Smail Ich slipped a hand under his armpit and helped him into the dark room where Sheikh Abbas was meditating after leading the prayers. It was a secluded room, built in haste, faintly lit by a high, narrow skylight. His head shaven and anointed, the sheikh was sitting cross-legged on a mat, a book crucified on a tiny stand. In his hand, a string of worry-beads clicked. Behind him, a stunted bookcase displayed a few hefty tomes, that was all: there was no chair, stool, not a pot or even a small carafe; just bare walls and, stuck in a corner, a flimsy incense stick was burning, sending up imperceptible wisps of smoke.

'Smail coughed into his fist to attract the master's attention, and backed out of the room. Abbas did not look up. He pointed to a corner of the mat. Kada dragged himself over to the designated spot and crumpled to his knees. The page of the book turned with a slight trembling. The sheikh calmly carried on reading, then said:

"Where did you get to, son of the Hilals?"

Kada retracted his head into his shoulders.

"I don't know."

"We've been trying to find you for weeks. Did you vanish under a spell?"

"I was hurt and I was furious. For days and nights, I walked without looking back. I wanted to disappear. I wanted to die."

Sheikh Abbas marked his page with the ribbon attached to the binding, and closed his book. He stared at his pupil long and hard, before stretching out his hand to raise his chin.

Kada recoiled in shame:

"Don't sully your hands on my impure flesh, master. I feel so dirty."

"All men are dirty in one way or another. Only there are those who can be washed by a simple glass of water, and those who could not be purified by all the oceans of the earth."

Kada broke down with shame, his shoulders racked with sobs.

"I have sinned, master, I have sinned . . ."

"Nobody is infallible. There is no more moving forgiveness than that implored with fervour. I don't want to know how you have spent your days, if you are sincere."

The sheikh stretched his arm out again. His hand grasped Kada's bristly neck, and Kada hunched up for protection.

"Did you love her as much as that?"

Feeling Kada's body stiffen beneath his palm, the sheikh went on:

"I know all about it. Ghachimat doesn't have walls thick enough to hold all its secrets. I would however like you to know that there is no woman in the world worth shedding a single tear over. And Sarah is not the best of women. She is beautiful as illusions are tempting. If destiny has made her another man's wife, tell yourself that, in a way, yours has spared you. It's an ill wind that blows nobody any good . . . Love is a servile attitude, a subordinate function. It is a role that falls to the women to perform, to earn our indulgence. The human drama begins as soon as a man loves a woman, for he should only recompense her with a master's moderate satisfaction."

"I've loved her since my earliest childhood."

"But you're not a child any more. You must banish her from your thoughts. There are decent virgins in the village who have preserved their honour to the point of going unnoticed. You don't see them, and nor do the others, and it is best that way . . . Sarah is a shameless hussy, a succubus possessed countless times by depraved spirits. She walks bareheaded, showing her calves, and she speaks loudly in the street. If fate has removed a poisonous plant from your path, it is because Sarah is not worthy of being trampled by your foot."

Kada Hilal suffered as he listened to the sheikh speak thus of the woman he worshipped. He furtively wiped his nose on his hand.

"I need time to get over it, master. I would like to go far away from here. I don't feel able to get a grip on myself if I stay near her."

"We need you with us. The local elections are coming up. I want to make you mayor of Ghachimat."

"I *must* leave."

"Where do you want to go?"

"Anywhere, Alger, Sétif, Biskra. There are many of us now. The country already belongs to us. I'd be happy with anything: a sheikh's secretary, mosque manager, militiaman for the Cause . . ."

The sheikh realized that he would have to select another candidate for the post of mayor. He retreated behind his beard to think. His worry-beads began clicking between his fingers again.

"The FIS has sent volunteers to Afghanistan," begged Kada. "I'd like to redeem myself with a gun in my hand. Please, help me join the *Mujahedin*." The sheikh's eyes lit up. Kada immediately knew that he had touched a particularly raw nerve, that his straying from the straight and narrow over the last few weeks had already been forgiven.

The agreement arrived after about a month. Kada just had the time to cram a couple of shirts, a pair of baggy trousers and a few religious books into his bag. To his mother, who watched him, he did not say a word about his expedition. He left the house without a glance at the walls that had watched him grow up, without a wave to those who had cherished him.

Tej Osmane was waiting for him in the street, arrogant

in his Afghan-style cassock. They climbed into the car with a green standard on the roof and drove through the village followed by a pack of yelling brats. The peasant farmers sitting on the terrace of the café stopped their chatter and their baleful gaze followed the vehicle haloed in dust heading for the Xaviers' farm.

Shouts went up the minute the car turned into the gravel farmyard. The whole flock was there, febrile and enthralled. Kada stepped out. He felt as though he were treading on the eternal grass of the celestial gardens. The crowd descended on him, arms fighting to touch him, lips reaching out to kiss a fold of his robe, despite Tej's appeal for calm.

Abbas appeared on the threshold of the meeting room. His emblematic silhouette, emaciated as a result of asceticism and abstinence, calmed people down. He smiled: a crack had just opened, offering him a tiny glimpse of paradise. With a protective hand, he invited the emissary to approach.

"Remember we'll be with you wherever you go, worthy son of Ghachimat. We will strengthen your arm when it is numb with cold, lend you our vigilance to overcome the gruelling nights, and our prayers will vanquish the fury of the bullets to rekindle your anger. Go, Kada Hilal, go and tell the infidels that the Word cannot be silenced, that no straitjacket can contain the faith. Go and tell the world that here, valour is natural, that the call of the Jihad makes us leap over seas and continents with a single stride . . . Go, I bless you."

The sheikh placed his lips on the pupil's head. A convulsion rippled through the entire brotherhood and some went into an ecstatic trance.

A month later, the Islamic Salvation Front swept to

victory in the local elections. Most town halls displayed fundamentalist slogans on their façades. Ghachimat celebrated its
victory for seven days and seven nights amid a symphony of
ululation and belching rifles. In the streets, fanatical youths
paraded relentlessly, provoking the downhearted. In the
jubilating mosque, new faces emerged, proud of the bristles
beginning to adorn their cheeks, promising a hirsute beard.
A few Elders ended up aligning themselves behind the fanatical
youths, without being the least embarrassed. Versatility became
a virtue. They listened with infinite interest to the new gurus
haranguing the dogs and demons, and they nodded their
approval of the murderous words as they had once welcomed
the authorized Hadith.

The former mayor was ordered to vacate the premises
and to touch nothing. "We will detect your fingerprints all
the way to the scaffold," declared 'Smail Ich, thoroughly revo-
lutionary in his way of exercising his new duties as local
magistrate.

That was how they set about cleansing the environment;
sympathizers' posts were renewed, while the puppets of the
tottering regime were hounded out *manu militari*. Women
were forced to wear the *hijab*, and a beard was compulsory
for men. From under his plane tree, Dactylo watched the
village turning into a fortress, the good-naturedness of old
transformed into aggression, idleness giving birth to chaos,
and in the evening, when he went to contemplate by the
temple, the things of the night no longer confided their most
intimate secrets to him.

Chapter thirteen

Zane-the-dwarf was perched on the branch of a tree, his arms pinioned to his sides like a bird of prey. He had remained thus for an hour, without quivering. It was because the village brats used to set their dogs on his heels that as a child Zane had learned to seek shelter in the trees. Despite his disability, he scaled them as fast as a monkey and stayed hidden among the branches until the siege was lifted. To keep fatigue and terror at bay, Zane tried to think about something else. That was how he began to dream about being a bird. At first, people hated coming across him in this position. They would retrace their steps and make a sign to ward off ill fortune. Zane ignored them. They could call him a crow, throw stones at him, nothing affected him. With time, people realized that they could not blame Zane for every calamity, and they no longer took any notice of him.

Mourad's gang had retreated to the river bed where a swarm of midges buzzed ceaselessly. A lazy grass-snake slid between the stones, as silent as a streak. Below stood idle donkeys, their front legs hobbled. From the depths of the forest came the shouts of the Brothers practising hand-to-hand combat. Their war cries rang out through the countryside, spasmodically sending up dense clouds of sparrows.

Lyès noticed that his cigarette had burnt away between his fingers.

"Why are they making all that racket?" he grumbled. "They've won the local council elections, they're going to have the Assembly, so why all these manoeuvres?"

Zane suddenly slid down from his branch and lay down in front of the craftsman.

"Do you think they'll want me?"

"If you're able to fight with a sabre in one hand and a stool in the other, they'll take you on the spot."

"Why a stool?"

"To stand on, of course. Otherwise, how will you be able to cross swords with the enemy? You barely reach his flies."

"That's not funny," said Zane, flaring up like a wisp of straw.

Lyès raised himself on one elbow to look at the dwarf.

"Are you serious? Do you really want to join them?"

"You have to make sure you're on the winning side in time. Besides, they're not necessarily wrong. We're a nation that only responds to bullying. There's nothing better than a kick in the arse to shake us up. Just look around, since they took control, we no longer have to bribe the counter clerk or beg the nurse. They keep a tight rein on everything. Besides, they're fighting for Islam, and I'm a Muslim."

"So you were when you were robbing the poor old grannies in the city."

"Well, I'm not going to spend my whole life on the wrong path."

"Those fellows have got nothing to do with Islam. Dactylo says they're deviationists. They're making religion their Trojan Horse."

Zane pricked up his ears inquisitively.

"Is that what Dactylo said?"

"He also said that they want to instigate international fundamentalism under the leadership of the Iranians. Haven't you ever heard of Hasan-e Sabbah, a Persian nutter who went and seized the fortress of Alamut and founded the Assassins sect? The word Assassins comes from *assassyine* which means 'fundamentalist' in Arabic. He rampaged through the land spreading terror and attacking the powerful lords in their own fiefs. Then everything settled down. Later, when the Ottoman Empire collapsed like a house of cards, the Iranians tried to fill the vacancy and install a caliphate so as to interfere in the affairs of the Muslim countries and get their hands on their wealth and have a good time."

"Dactylo's never been outside the village," protested Zane. He can't know what's going on elsewhere."

"Dactylo's read heaps of books. You only have to listen to him spouting clever words that nobody can be bothered to look up in a dictionary. He's not a cretin like you."

"I'm not a cretin. We live in a democracy and I'm a fully fledged citizen," moaned Zane, rising. "I'm entitled to choose which side I want to be on."

"Who'd want a midget?"

Zane sniggered. He tapped his head.

"I'm small in stature, not in mind."

He spun round and rushed off over the fields. From the main street in the village, 'Smail Ich was supervising a road-mending crew who were filling in the pot-holes in the tarmac. Under the shelter of a tree, Issa Osmane and a group of old men were marvelling at the performance of a steam-roller. Tej's father claimed that the machine was quicker than a man, and the others learnedly nodded their heads. Zane went down a putrid-smelling alley to Tej Osmane's garage. The mechanic was changing a set of brake pads. Without stopping work, he asked:

"Problems?"

Zane shrugged and squatted in front of the vehicle.

"Let me join your team."

"You don't know anything about mechanics."

"I mean the other team. I say my prayers and I've stopped stealing. The other day, I found a purse and I gave it back to its owner without looking inside. What more must I do to be recruited?"

"You already are."

"How come?"

"You keep an eye open for trouble."

Zane wasn't thrilled. He kept his head down and his hands on his knees.

"I need exercise. I want to wear the white armband

with green writing on it too, and parade in front of the crowds, wave banners and shout 'death to the traitors' from the rooftops."

"Walls have ears ... there's some coffee in the Thermos."

Zane waddled like a duck, filled a cup and came back, his buttocks scraping the ground. Tej adjusted the pads and stepped back to position the wheel.

Zane blurted out:

"Dactylo's got a big mouth. He can talk the hind leg off a donkey."

"Really?"

"He says this nutter lived on the mountain and founded the assassins who were the fundamentalists. I think he's got it in for Sheikh Abbas. He also said that the Persians and the Iranians are behind all this to bring back this fellow Otman Nemper from Mecca and make him caliph because he's rich, and then we'll all be able to have a good time."

"What on earth are you on about?"

"Well Lyès used French words and I found it hard to follow him. One thing's certain, Dactylo can't stand us."

Tej fitted the wheel, let down the jack and tightened the wheel nuts. He stood up, took a handful of banknotes from his pocket and gave two to Zane.

"In the meantime, go and have a good time."

The money vanished into Zane's pocket as if by magic. But he didn't leave.

"Now what?"

Zane swallowed, took a deep breath, and enquired:

"I just want to know: is it because of my size?"

"Your eyes and ears are enough for us. Now go away. I've got to change a cylinder head gasket."

Jafer eventually faced the facts: he had to get used to it. His friends had left, each going their own way. Allal Sidhom was forever in a hurry to get back to his wife. Dactylo couldn't stand him any more. The café was like an old people's home, the village like a barracks. The Brothers were gradually carrying out an inquisition; they were all over the place, intimidating people, pressurizing them. Jafer didn't know where he was. He swung from one extreme to another. At night, he swore he would leave the village at first light; during the day he realized he had neither the strength nor the guts to venture further than Moulay Naim. And eventually, exhaustion broke his will like a rotten yoke. One day, his father looked up from his digging to discover him standing in the middle of the field, a cap on his head and a pick in his hand.

"What do you want?"

"Can't you see? I've come to give you a hand."

"You don't work with a pick, but with the heart," said his father, going back to his labours.

Jafer was disconcerted. He'd been expecting a more enthusiastic reception.

"You were angry with me because I didn't do anything. Now I'm behaving you tell me to get lost."

His father spun round, his face livid with rage:

"Your grandfather loved this land with a passion. He adored every ear of corn, and he spent the best part of his time watching his corn growing a millimetre at a time, until it was as tall as him. At the age of eighty, he dragged the plough with the strength of two oxen. Not once, in spite of all the droughts, did he think of mortgaging it. When he strutted about his fields, holding an armful of sheaves, it was the whole world he was grasping. Me too, I cursed when he dragged me from my marriage bed at all hours. But in the end I understood. When the Agrarian Revolution amputated a large portion of our land, when the socialist tractors uprooted our almond trees, your grandfather sat on the edge of the well over there, clutched his heart and fell stone dead. And you, because your friends have dropped you, you grab your pick, you come here, and you think quite naturally that it's enough to work the ground to deserve it . . . Go back where you came from, Jafer. Think quietly, crumble a handful of earth between your fingers, again and again. The day you feel its pulse, when you are certain that it breathes a little of its life into you, join us and we will welcome you with open arms."

The horizon bled purple that night, but Jafer remained oblivious. He stayed behind in the fields, long after his father and brothers had departed, leaning on his pick, then sitting in a furrow, his head between his knees, completely indistinguishable from the scarecrows to anyone passing in the distance.

Chapter fourteen

Dactylo frowned. It was the second time that the two municipal trucks were driving up from the other side of the hill. Laden with gravel and sand in the morning, now they were back carrying hundreds of bags of cement and iron rollers. Over the hill was the water tower, but that had already been rebuilt. Dactylo scratched his head wondering what on earth could require such a huge operation.

His customer, a small man with a goatee beard like an evil spirit, also turned to look at the convoy.

"They're building an irrigation lake," he explained in the hope of seeing the letter-writer get back to work.

Dactylo let out a "hmm!", banged at his keyboard, corrected a mistake and continued the sentence to the end of the line. The customer craned his neck, impressed by the Roman letters that were printed as if by magic. His turban trailed on the keyboard. Without showing any irritation, Dactylo waited patiently until the man moved back and let him finish the job.

"So, you're thinking of selling your aunt's house . . . ?"

The customer was disconcerted for a moment, as if the public letter-writer had just put his finger on a secret, then he nodded:

"Tell him that Aunt Zohra decided by herself to get rid of her hovel. She will live with my children, in my house. She'll have all she needs to eat and will do as she pleases. Don't they say that when times are hard, that's when families rally round?"

The machine rapped out three lines and then stopped.

"Yes? . . ."

"What? Have you explained?"

"Of course."

"That was very quick. Look carefully. You must have forgotten to mention one important detail."

Remaining cheerful in the face of adversity, Dactylo reread the last three lines.

"You see," cried his customer. "I told you. You forgot to emphasize 'get rid of'. GET RID OF."

Dactylo inserted his customer's amendment, a little annoyed at being an accessory to a dubious operation. But that was part of the job. He knew other public letter-writers who were all ears and kept records to blackmail their customers as a way of making ends meet. He removed the sheet from the typewriter, carefully folded it in four, slid it into an envelope and held it out to the customer.

"That's thirty dinars."

100

The man protested before paying, then he walked away swearing that in future he'd go to another, less greedy letter-writer.

'Smail Ich parked his service car outside the café. His five young children were arguing on the back seat. He ordered them to be good, slammed the door and tightened his belt round his *kamis*, wriggling his behind. First of all his sweeping, menacing gaze intimidated a group of old men sitting apart under a porch before lighting on the peasant farmers sitting at the tables on the pavement. Some of them hastily shifted their position. Behind the bar, Ammar put on an attentive smile, extricated a suitable cup from the dishwater, wiped it on his apron and put it to one side in case he needed it.

'Smail had acquired sufficient authority since being appointed mayor. He was no longer the despised lout with a ridiculous laugh. He had learned to walk with a measured pace, to smile with moderation, and to shun familiarity. Of course, his beard was still repulsive, but he continued to divest himself of his coarse rural ways so as to be able to fulfil his new role. He stopped people he met, asked them how they were, and wrote down their grievances in a little notebook. No other mayor had ever done that before. "Responsibility is a burden, not a privilege," he loved to say.

He said to a farmer sitting by the café door:

"I hear you've had a baby."

"A daughter," lamented the father.

"Is it the sixth?"

"The ninth, Mr Mayor, sir. Nothing but girls."

"Well, you're going to have to make your mind up: either you get a new wife or you get a new pair of testicles!"

A burst of laughter greeted the mayor's joke, despite the farmer's disgruntled look.

'Smail touched the hands of two old acquaintances and went up to a timid old man:

"You should be having a nap, Kouider. Otherwise how will you be able to do your job as night watchman?"

The old man didn't wait to be told twice. He picked up his bludgeon and disappeared. Two others, sensing that their absenteeism would get them into trouble, tiptoed away.

"Well, well, Sy Rabah, I thought you were in Sidi Bel Abbes."

"I'm waiting for the bus. It's three hours late."

'Smail scribbled in his notebook.

"I'm going to sort out this transport problem once and for all. You'll have a bus three times a day."

The mayor's promise was greeted with a clamour of relief and gratitude, and 'Smail relished every last quaver.

In the street, he admired the main road with its new asphalt surface, the splendid street lamps, the town hall daubed in bright colours, the green calligraphy on the pediment then, in the distance, the three municipal trucks returning from the construction site. He thumped his fist against his other hand as a sign of pride, clenching it tighter when his glance fell on Dactylo.

"How's business going, letter-writer?"

"The same as things in general."

"Everything is going very well," retorted 'Smail touchily.

"Good."

'Smail was wary. He knew Dactylo was enigmatic, and was afraid of being made to look a fool by some subtle play on words.

"With you, there's always something fishy going on."

"The river's dried up, 'Smail."

"Mr Mayor to you! Don't be so familiar . . . With you one never knows what's in your head."

"Only my brain."

"I've heard you can't stand us."

"From whom?"

"I've got my eye on you. Watch out."

'Smail took a few steps away then swung on his heel:

"By the way, what's your real name, Dactylo? It's annoying not to know after all this time. You must have done something pretty bad if you're so afraid to tell us. Unless it's got obscene connotations?"

He spoke in a monotone, but his words hit home, full of menace. Dactylo felt a sudden wrench in his gut.

For the third time, the municipal trucks devoured the dusty track up the hill. More and more intrigued, Dactylo put away his apparatus under the plane tree and decided to go up and investigate.

A huge construction site had been set up around the temple. Dozens of volunteers were teeming in the blazing heat in a dance of groaning wheelbarrows and carts. They were digging up the age-old flagstones, digging trenches in the centre of the temple, brutally ravaging the historic site. Dactylo darted from one operation to another, begging them to stop

the massacre, then, horrified, he rushed up to Tej Osmane,
who was supervising the works from the top of a mound.

"You must stop this vandalism at once."

Tej ignored him. He continued shouting at the strag-
glers. Dactylo made a furious grab at his shoulder:

"I'm talking to you."

Tej glared menacingly at the offending hand, and
pushed it away with contempt:

"Next time, I'll cut it off at the wrist and stuff it in
your big mouth."

"You're destroying the temple."

"What temple? These rotten old ruins? We're going to
build a monumental mosque here, and just look at the view
we'll have over the valley . . . Now, give me some air. We
need it around here."

Dactylo realized that he would get nowhere with Tej.
He began to run like a madman towards the Xaviers' farm.
The sheikh's militiamen stopped him at the entrance.

"I want to see Abbas."

"He's meditating."

"It's urgent."

Boudjema, Mourad's brother, stared at the public letter-
writer.

"All right. I'll go and see what I can do."

He returned within a few minutes.

"What's it about?"

"The temple. They're demolishing it."

"Ah, I see."

Dactylo had to wait an hour before being conducted
before the sheikh.

"I'm listening."

"Sheikh, you've got to stop the destruction of the temple."

"Why?"

"What do you mean, why? It's an historic site, our heritage . . ."

"And what is its history?"

"I don't know. The ruins are hundreds of years old, probably thousands. And they've survived wars, erosion . . . we must preserve them. They are priceless evidence. They're part of our history."

"They were there before us. So they don't belong to us."

"They belong to History."

"Mythology!" snapped the sheikh. "True History began with the advent of Islam."

"There were other religions before, other prophets. The Holy Scriptures dedicate a number of important chapters to them."

"I forbid you to bring the Book into your drunken ramblings!"

The sheikh went back to his reading. The interview was over. Boudjema seized the public letter-writer by the arm and threw him out.

Chapter fifteen

"I'm relieved to hear you're working with your father," said Allal Sidhom.

Jafer wasn't listening to him. He was looking around the living-room, which no longer had shabby walls, nor tattered curtains, even less the stench of poverty that used to pervade his friend's house. The walls were gay with new wallpaper, there was a carpet on the floor and there were pretty curtains at the windows. One corner was illuminated by a little aquarium full of tiny fish, with a lead underwater diver standing guard over a chest that opened and closed, letting out an endless stream of air bubbles.

"I say, you're living in the lap of luxury."

"It doesn't take much."

Jafer's gaze wandered over all the fine things brought by Sarah. On the opposite wall, was a portrait of the couple, photographed on the morning after their wedding night. Sarah looked sublime in her bridal gown, with long gloves coming up to her elbows. She was holding a bouquet of paper flowers. Allal had the smile of a man who can't believe his happiness. His tie was askew, but his suit impeccable.

"Happy?"

"Overjoyed," said Allal blushing.

Jafer was both jealous and touched.

"You're a good person, Allal. I'm pleased for you."

"Thank you."

"When are you going to introduce me to your wife?"

"You know very well it's not the done thing."

"Don't make a fuss. I want to see her close up."

"She wouldn't come. She's very modest."

"She went to high school, didn't she? She knows what it's all about."

Allal gave in. He went to fetch his wife. Jafer heard him imploring her, laughing, and her shyly refusing to follow him. "Are you crazy? It isn't done . . ." At last, the door opened, and Sarah appeared like the dawn. Jafer was embarrassed. Now that she was there in front of him, he was confused and felt stupid.

"It's Happy-go-lucky," said Allal, holding his wife's arm to stop her from running away. "He's crafty and I can't do without him."

Jafer held out his hand, and withdrew it at once. His throat dry, he heard himself stutter:

"Does this lout treat you well?"

Sarah let out a little giggle. To Jafer, it sounded like a stream burbling in the forest.

"You see?" Allal reproached him jokingly, releasing his wife. "She's afraid of you."

Sarah vanished like a bright spot in the mist.

"There. Now you've seen her."

"Not enough."

"Watch it! Sit down and tell me what it's like, working the land."

Jafer stared at the spot where Sarah had stood.

"Hey, do you hear me?"

"God, she's beautiful. Would you exchange her for an eye? I'd have to keep one to admire her."

"That's enough. You'll bring the evil eye on us."

Jafer calmed down and went back to his seat.

"So, tell me about the fields."

"It hasn't been easy, but I'm getting used to it. My father let me stew for a fortnight before accepting me. I don't have trouble sleeping at night any more. How's life as a cop?"

"The fundamentalists are giving us a hard time."

"I know. Things are going downhill. I don't like it. What is it they want? They've got the local councils . . ."

Allal raised his glass to his lips and put it down again to say:

"They say that the FIS has given the order for civil disobedience."

"Meaning . . . ?"

"I don't know. But it's bound to be nasty."

"Are things really as bad as all that?"

"In Alger, it's a disaster. The riot police have been mobilized. Every day, they have to disperse the demonstrators with tear gas. A powder-keg's been lit and it's all going to blow up any minute now."

"Stop, you frighten me."

"I'm frightened too, you know. The first tile to come loose will land on my head. The fundamentalists are busy forming an alternative army. You should see them parading through the streets like paras. There are things going on in the woods. The Sidi Said quarry reported the theft of a large quantity of explosives."

"Maybe it's subversion."

Allal shook his head:

"Last week a woman and her six-year-old son were burned alive in their home. The mother was accused of prostitution. Similar attacks have been reported elsewhere. On Friday, after prayer, the crowd specifically goes down streets where there is a police station, chanting 'No democracy, no Constitution, only the Sunna and the Koran' . . ."

Allal suddenly stopped and sat up. There were shouts outside, followed by a commotion. People could be heard coming out onto their verandas, and then into the street.

Ghachimat was in turmoil. The news struck like a bomb on a mosque. The horde of Brothers was out in force, grief-stricken. Then Tej Osmane climbed up onto the minaret, his face flushed, and cried:

"Brothers, our leaders have been arrested. The members of the Majlis are all in gaol. And so is Sheikh Abbas."

Chapter sixteen

It was Jelloul-the-fool who saw it first. He was sprawled in a tangle of grass watching the ants when the taxi drew up before the bridge. Jelloul sat up. Saliva drooled down his chin dropping elastic gobbets onto his chest. The man paid the driver, then embraced the mountain, the hill and the valley with his gaze. He seemed in a hurry to conquer them. A kit-bag slung over his shoulder, he marched valiantly on the village.

Jelloul did not recognize him straight away because of his rig-out: a turban with a kind of khaki cap on top, jacket down to the knees, oriental robes underneath, then thick socks coming out of a grotesque pair of shoes halfway between clodhoppers and hiking boots. The man turned towards the madman and smiled at him. Only then did Jelloul realize who he was:

"*Wah Wah,* Kada . . . Kada . . ."

Kada Hilal could have been dropped off at his house. If he asked the taxi to stop at the bridge, it was to show the villagers, big and small, that he was back from Afghanistan, without a scratch, but his head still ringing with the sound of bullets.

Hadji Baroudi paused in the middle of his ablutions and took a long time to put a name to the tanned face staring at him.

"The son of the Hilals is back," he said, pushing away his pot.

The news spread round the village in a twinkling. Clusters of kids, then whole swarms of them began to gather behind the returned soldier. The old men who had been dozing in the shade elbowed each other awake. Zane-the-dwarf jumped down from his perch, let out a yell and ran to Kada, hampering his progress, his incongruous appearance detracting from the martial solemnity of the man whom Sheikh Abbas had elevated to the rank of martyr, just over a year earlier.

"The hero's back!"

Intrigued by the noise, Tej Osmane came out of his garage. The sight of his friend made him take a step back. He quickly washed his hands in a trough and rushed towards the crowd.

"God be praised! You've come back to us alive."

And they collided in an emotional embrace.

The crowd became impossible to control, the Brothers hit out with their coshes to clear the way for the *Mujahed* of the Orient. The throng grew even more excited, bursting into religious chants which rang through the streets. 'Smail Ich –

who had slightly lost face since his dismissal after the dissolution of the FIS – arrived sobbing, his paunch wobbling. Zane climbed onto a low wall and, cupping his hands around his mouth, acted the muezzin. The procession entered the square, spilling out of the courtyard of the town hall and forcing Dactylo hastily to gather up his belongings.

"That's enough," panted Tej. "You'll suffocate him."

The Brothers started getting rough. At one point, the returned hero lost patience and hit a youth. Actually, his gaze had just fallen on Sarah's house.

People calmed down in front of the Hilals' residence. Kada raised his arm to request silence. Those lagging behind carried on yelling. Those in front turned round to ask them to be quiet, and thus, from one row to another, the outburst of enthusiasm simmered down; even the children were quiet.

"Thank you for your welcome, brothers," said Kada, wiping away a tear. "It's the most wonderful present I've ever had. May God bless you."

There was uproar. One voice rose above the general hubbub shouting that the *Mujahed* was the long-awaited *Mehdi*. Kada thanked him humbly and went into his house. Once again, the chants rose up, fervent as prayers and inflexible as oaths.

For a week, Kada remained buried in his books, tolerating neither his mother's fussing nor his sisters' prying. At night, he went out into the garden and talked to himself. In the morning, he monopolized the veranda, where he read or drafted manifestos. During this time, nobody in the vicinity was allowed to move. In the afternoon, he allowed his friends to visit. They sat around drinking tea and chatting in the shadow of the reeds. He told them about his battles, the ambushes he had set, the heavy losses he had inflicted on the enemy, the Soviet armada that was so weak confronted with the faith of the *Mujahedin*. The Brothers waited stoically for him to regain his breath before telling him about the government's trickery, how the electoral process had been flouted, the leaders of the Islamic movement arrested, the concentration camps where their comrades had been handed over to the mercy of the desert and their torturers . . .

"The police raided us in the middle of the night," Boudjema told him indignantly, "crammed us like cattle into paddy wagons and deported some of us to Reggane and others to Im Emguel, in the hope we'd be wiped out by sunstroke."

"We cleaned up the majority vote," Tej Osmane reminded them. "The Guemmar affair was fabricated to discredit us in the eyes of the public, but it failed. They arrested the entire Majlis to confuse us. But the people weren't fooled by their tricks. The *Jihad* has begun in the Alger region. Police, infidels and collaborators are killed every day by our bullets."

"I've seen, I've seen," replied Kada, full of self-importance. "News of the war here reached us even in the remotest areas of Lashkar Gah."

Tej could barely contain himself. Kada was disappointing. They talked to him about Blida, and he immediately started talking about Chaghcharan. They listed the attacks carried out in Boufarik, and he told them about his exploits in the Hindu Kush. He did not seem to understand that the Brothers had come to him to swear allegiance and make him face up to his responsibilities. Sheikh Abbas was no longer there, and it was up to him, Kada Hilal, the valiant *Mujahed* of the Salang pass, to declare holy war in the region.

It took Tej Osmane a month to wake up to who he was.

Chapter seventeen

The imam Hadji Salah lay on his side, his hands clasped under his chin, unable to get to sleep. He listened to the rattling of the rickety windows battered by the wind. Outside, the rain spluttered ineffectively on the hill intermittently streaked with flashes of lightning. Sometimes, the lightning struck nearby and the room was lit up with a dazzling flash, giving the shadows monstrous forms.

"Why aren't you asleep?" asked his elderly wife.

"Because of the thunder."

Hadji Salah had been unable to sleep since he had resumed his duties as imam. He had found the mosque disaster-stricken. It was difficult to turn an arena into a prayer hall even if, initially, it had been built for meditation. When the demon is exorcized, the possessed victim still remains weakened. The scant congregation took no notice of his religious service. They came to escape the boredom and the oppressive heat. The few young people openly showed their hostility to all that was not extremist. They missed the virulence of the sermons, the sound and the fury. Also, when Hadji Salah ascended the *minbar*, his voice irritated them and many of them only attended one Friday a month.

The situation was growing steadily worse. Farmers were being robbed of their guns by hooded individuals, travellers were attacked on the roads, and nobody dared go to a neighbour's bedside after nightfall. Families were torn apart by quarrels. Hadji Boudali had sunk into total insanity and they had been forced to lock him up in an asylum.

Hadji Salah was worried and furious with himself. He did not understand why, when he stood at the *minbar*, his indignation deserted him and the words stuck in his throat.

"Someone's knocking at the door," said his wife.

Hadji Salah had heard. He pushed back the blanket and rummaged under the bed for his slippers.

"It's bound to be Dahou," he reassured her. "Every time there's a storm at night, he rouses the whole village."

The wife watched her husband slip on his robe, cover his head with a towel and go out onto the patio.

"Forgive us for kidnapping you in such a casual manner," said Kada.

"So it's a kidnapping, is it," said the imam bitterly.

He did not know how many hours he had lain there, his face on the floor, in the back of the van, nor how he had managed to walk through the forest, his hands bound and his eyes blindfolded, until they reached this hut where those who had ordered his capture were waiting. Four men were staring at him with grave expressions. Kada Hilal sat on a cushion, his face impassive. Next to him, Tej Osmane was mechanically stroking the blade of a machete. 'Smail Ich was leaning against the wall, his hands clasped over his stomach. The fourth was a pale, puny boy, almost lost in his voluminous para jacket. He had a fringe of down on the tip of his chin and venom in his eyes. It was Yusef, Hadji Boudali's son.

"Sit down on the stool."

The imam preferred a straw mat.

"You could have asked me to follow you, and I would have done so. And my wife would not be going frantic at this hour. She's a diabetic."

"You'll be returned to her before dawn," promised Kada.

Tej fidgeted impatiently:

"Tell him why he's here."

Kada calmed him with a lofty gesture.

He turned to the imam:

"Hadji Salah, you are a good man. That is why we are appealing to you. It's true, we have not been gentle with the Elders. But not in any way out of arrogance. The world is changing and they refuse to recognize it ... Since Independence, our country has been permanently regressing. Our natural resources have sapped our convictions and our efforts. Traitors have amused themselves luring us with false promises. They have introduced us to jingoistic vanities and demagogy. For thirty years, they've been taking us for a ride. Result: the country is a disaster, young people are apathetic, hope gone.

Everywhere people are giving up. Worse, having lost our identity, now we're losing our soul."

Kada stopped. Sheikh Abbas always used to stop in that
way, suddenly, to make his audience sit up.

"We say 'that's enough!'"

'Smail Ich nodded:

"That's enough."

"That was how the Movement was born. It is God
who inspired the Islamic Salvation Front. He took pity
on this disconcerted nation under threat of destruction from
a bunch of phoneys through abuses of trust and authority,
outrageous nepotism, blatant incompetence and corruption.
We had the most beautiful country in the world, and they've
turned it into a pig-sty. We had a certain historic legitimacy, they have usurped it. And they have undermined all
our prospects for the future . . . That is why we say 'that's
enough'."

"That's enough," echoed 'Smail looking preoccupied.

"We members of the FIS have behaved decently. We
have worked and shown what we are capable of. The people
voted for our principles and our ideology. But the thugs in
power refuse to face up to the facts. They have deliberately
chosen to play with fire. That's why we're now offering them
the fires of hell."

Hadji Salah looked up in the silence that had fallen
over the hut. Tej had cut his finger on the blade of the
machete. Yusef now had two blazing embers beneath his
brow. Only 'Smail carried on nodding.

"And it's war," said Kada.

"It's war," repeated 'Smail.

Hadji Salah was tired. He was growing drowsy but the sharp pains in his joints kept him awake.

"What exactly do you want of me, son of the Hilals?"

"A *fatwa.*"

"I don't have the requisite learning. I'm just a rural imam whose modest knowledge is diminishing and whose memory is increasingly unreliable."

"You have been the village imam for forty years," cut in Tej exasperated by Kada's emphatic and excessive loquaciousness. "You are fair and enlightened. We want you to declare a holy war."

"And who is the enemy?"

"All those who wear uniform: police, the army . . ."

"Even postmen," said 'Smail sarcastically, instantly undermining the solemnity that Kada had so carefully contrived to impress the imam.

Hadji Salah remained silent for a moment, lying prostrate, his head in his hands, as if he refused to believe what he had just heard. The moment he had been dreading had come. The beast had awoken within the child who no longer understood why, suddenly, the urge to punish was stronger than that to forgive. The poet was right: there was inevitably a share for the Devil in every religion that God offered man; a tiny share, but largely sufficient to falsify the Message and lead the unwary astray down the path of evil and barbarism. That Devil's share is ignorance. Sidi Saim used to say: "There are three things it is against nature to entrust to the ignorant man: wealth would cause him suffering; power would turn him into a tyrant, and religion would be equally damaging to him and to others."

Hadji Salah shivered. At first, there had been the mercy of God, who was aware of the trials and tribulations that confronted the most accomplished as well as the most vulnerable of His creatures, those born into pain, who owe their survival only to a bitter struggle, from their first steps to their last breath. But men do not know how to read the Signs. They interpret them to suit themselves. They turn dreams into a utopia, light into pyres, and they become unjust and foolish.

Hadji Salah feebly surfaced from his state of confusion. He didn't have the strength to wipe his streaming face with his hand. He stared in turn at Kada, Tej, Yusef and 'Smail and said:

"Do you know why God commanded Abraham to sacrifice his beloved son?"

"Of course."

"Why?"

"To test Abraham's faith," said Yusef.

"Blasphemy! Do you dare insinuate that God doubted His prophet? Is he not the All-knowing? . . . God simply had a message for all the nations. By asking Abraham to kill his son on top of the mountain, and then offering him a ram in place of the child, He wanted to make men understand that Faith has its limits too, that it stops when a man's life is threatened. For God *knows* the value of life. That is the seat of all His benevolence."

The canvas bag was placed in the middle of the bridge so that it would be seen by the first person to pass that way. It was covered with buzzing flies. The stench had put the birds to flight. Jelloul was in a state of shock. Something had flashed through his tormented mind and jogged a memory from long, long ago. He pictured himself as a child, clad in a patched tunic. It was a rainy morning in the winter of 1959. Jelloul was taking lunch to his father, a groom at the Xavier's. On the bridge, he had found a bag, just like the one there now, out of which poked a human head. Because he didn't really understand, because he could neither run away nor scream, Jelloul had sunk into madness.

This new canvas bag on the bridge also contained a man's decapitated head. That of the imam Hadji Salah. Jelloul raised his hands to his temples and began to howl and howl . . .

Chapter eighteen

Only a few people turned out for the funeral. Many judged it prudent to stay away so as not to expose themselves. The Elders were pale, speechless. Muffled in their robes, they looked like ghosts. The funeral address was interspersed with long silences. When the gravedigger placed the imam's head in the grave, Hadji Menouar collapsed at the feet of Hadji Maurice, and nobody bothered to help him up.

At the end of the ceremony, a boy asked his father why the Islamists had attacked a religious man. His father replied: "A good believer begins with himself."

The rest of the corpse was only found a month later on Djebel el Khouf, devoured by jackals.

Ghachimat did not have time to dry its tears. The same night, the postmaster was kidnapped from his home. An armed gang forced him to hand over the money and stamps, then they hanged him and set the place on fire.

The reign of terror had begun. The valley entered into a different world, a world of atrocities. The rutting sun did not rid the days of the pervading darkness. Night fell like a treacherous, greedy ogress tracking down people and noises, and everybody went to earth and kept silent. Fear fed on the news: the factory in Moulay Naim had been burned down; the police station at Hassi Meskhout had been blown up by a home-made bomb; the roads were no longer safe, mausoleums had been destroyed and cemeteries desecrated . . .

Habib-the-hairdresser's son had had his throat slit at Moulay Naim. He had been on leave. Zane-the-dwarf had seen him alight from the taxi and had signalled to 'Smail Ich. The reservist was intercepted that same evening, as he left the hammam. Yusef, the son of Hadji Boudali, said to him: "You did well to have a good scrub. That'll save us having to wash your body." At first the reservist thought it was a joke. Yusef was his childhood friend. They had been circumcised on the same day and by the same taleb . . . He died on his feet, taken unawares, clutching his severed neck. His father found him lying on the road, naked and mutilated. Oddly, the street was empty. Nobody had seen or heard a thing. Habib buried his boy at the cemetery in Moulay Naim, surrounded by his family and a few acquaintances visibly reluctant to be there. To one relative he said: "If he'd been killed in a fight, with his gun in his hand, I could have accepted it. But they killed him at home, unarmed and without warning, and that, I can't forgive." Zane was there, offering his condolences. He faithfully reported the immoderate grief of the hairdresser, who was decapitated, three days later, in his salon.

And yet, after the terror of the first tragedies, Ghachimat was full of surprises. Dactylo was expecting to see people react, or at least condemn the horrors. Little by little, in the café, at the market, in the mosque, the dread gave way to amusement. People began to find the spectacular attacks had panache, the murderers a thrilling recklessness, the executions a "legitimacy". When, one morning, the charred body of Maza-the-janitor was found among the smouldering carcases in the town car park, people remarked, to anyone who cared to listen, that Maza had been perfectly disagreeable to the mountain-dwellers who turned up at the town hall, that he had been corrupt, and that in view of the humiliations he used to inflict on poor Issa Osmane, he fully deserved his punishment. And when, in Moulay Naim, Dahmane, an elderly retired policeman, was found hanging in a cowshed, everyone was quick to enumerate the excesses and abuses he had accumulated during his career as "mob breaker".

"Those with a clear conscience can sleep soundly," people told themselves. "The people who've been killed weren't all angels."

Spring enchanted neither beast nor man. The poppies evoked burst blisters. The left section of the cemetery would soon reach the opposite walls. Every day, a convoy consigned its dear departed to the earth that had become a mass grave.

One night, Allal Sidhom ventured home. Zane caught him slipping furtively along the prickly pear hedge, like a thief. "Don't stay there, cop. *They* might catch you and that'll be the end of you." Then, on seeing Allal's disappointment: "OK, seeing as you're here, you can stay for the night, only promise me you won't leave your house. There are spies around. If it looks like there's going to be a ruckus, I'll let you know. Otherwise, try and clear off before dawn." Allal hesitated. "It's not worth it. I'm leaving now. Don't tell anyone I came." Allal retraced his steps and vanished. Zane stayed put. He went and hid a few metres away and did not take his eyes off the house. Within the hour, Allal was back, almost crawling. Zane let him go into his house and ran to alert Yusef whose job was to execute the village *taghout* and who regularly patrolled the area ready to intervene the minute an undesirable was spotted.

Around three o'clock in the morning, Sarah was awakened by a scraping sound. She went over to the window and caught sight of two shadows climbing over the patio wall. Allal just had time to slip on his trousers and flee out of the back. Shots pursued him through the narrow streets. He retaliated blindly, heard one of the assailants howl and set off across the fields as if possessed.

Kada Hilal was beside himself. He paced furiously up and down the hut which served as his HQ on the top of Djebel el-Khouf. Yusef stood to attention, pale but upright. Tej Osmane was carving a piece of wood with his pen-knife, his buttocks resting on a jerry can and his foot against a beam. Outside, 'Smail Ich was showing the new recruits how to dismantle and reassemble an army rifle taken from a soldier killed in an ambush.

"You let him slip between your fingers!" fumed Kada. "Seven against one and he manages to wound one of you and vanish into thin air."

"We must have hit him."

"But you're not certain."

"We need proper weapons. Our old shotguns don't have a very long range."

"If you'd wiped out Allal you'd be wearing his pistol in your belt as a trophy," retorted Tej, snapping shut his pen-knife.

Kada dismissed Yusef and his group. He asked to be left alone. The crew backed away. Tej closed the door behind them and turned to the emir.

"They did what they could."

"I don't think it's enough. I want that bastard's head."

Tej sat on a stool and crossed his legs on the table, his soles facing the "Afghan". He examined his nails ostentatiously.

"I'll bring it to you on a platter," he promised. "Neatly sliced off and dripping with blood."

Through the window, Kada gazed at a herd of lambs grazing, and the few stolen cars that made up his unit's fleet, the tents skilfully camouflaged under the branches and the bound prisoner at the foot of a tree.

"What are you waiting for to execute that scum?"

"We're prolonging the agony."

"Did he say anything?"

"He's a newly enlisted reservist. He didn't have the time to learn his sergeant's name."

Kada stared at the prisoner, a puny boy, barely into his

teens, who had not stopped shivering since his capture during a fake roadblock.

"I want Allal's head."

"You'll have his head, and the *rest*."

Kada frowned.

"Meaning . . . ?"

Tej rose and planted himself in front of the emir:
"Sarah."

Kada made to protest, but his lieutenant's frosty expression dissuaded him.

Intrigued by the gathering outside the mosque, a mountain-dweller alighted from his donkey and went up to a young man absorbed by the posters the fundamentalists had pasted on the wall of the sanctuary.

"What do they say?"

Zane craned his neck to identify the mountain-dweller, an old man with an emaciated face and large, coarse hands.

"That," said the dwarf pointing at the poster on the left, "is the list of prizes. And that's the names of the lottery winners."

"Ah," said the mountain-dweller none the wiser.

The left-hand poster began with an authorized hadith and listed all the practices that were strictly banned. In addition to the original taboos, the faithful were to abstain from modern sins such as the Turkish bath, beauty salons, wearing a skirt, make-up, music, the practice of clairvoyance, the consumption of tobacco, reading and selling newspapers, the satellite dish, games of chance, beaches etc.

On the right-hand poster, after a verse from the Koran scrawled in a clumsy hand, was the list of people murdered by the fundamentalists and the reasons for their killing. Alongside the names were the words *taghout, traitor, harki, enemy.*

The killing had already been going on for two years. After eliminating the government "henchmen", their collaborators and recalcitrants, the barbarism had spread its tentacles more or less everywhere. *Fellahin,* elementary schoolteachers, shepherds, night-watchmen and children were all executed with indescribable savagery. People began to find the reckless deeds of the Islamists less and less thrilling. They realized that it was always the downtrodden who were killed, that absolutely nobody was exempt. Little girls were kidnapped, raped and dismembered in the woods. Boys were recruited by force and indoctrinated. Shopkeepers were subjected to extortion. The idle were unwittingly recruited. First of all they became lookouts, then harbourers, and then finally, without warning, they woke up with a gun in their hands. By the time they realized what had happened to them, it was too late: their finger had already squeezed the trigger.

Kada Hilal took a deep breath. Tej Osmane was right. When he first saw himself at the head of some thirty volunteers, half of whom vanished at the first clashes with the authorities, he was on the point of laying down his arms and fleeing abroad. But Tej was keeping an eye out for trouble. The losses made him neither weaken nor give up. He said: "Whatever you do, don't despair, my dear emir. We have thousands of recruits. They are waiting for us along the walls, in the cafés, amid the disarray and discontent. All they are waiting for is a sign to mobilize them. Even if they don't believe in our ideology, when they become aware of the danger they represent, of the loot to be collected, when they realize that the lives and possessions of others belong to them, each one of them will find he is a little god ... Poverty doesn't believe in havens of peace. Unleash it and you will see it hurl itself at the fortune of others. If you want to back a monster that will prove sturdy, choose it among the most deprived. Suddenly it will dream of an empire full of slaughterhouses and whores and, from then on, if it had wings, it would try to take Satan's place."

Chapter nineteen

"You ought to try and bring your brother back," Dactylo told Mourad. "He's a good boy. His place is with his family."

Mourad shrugged.

"I can't do anything for him. I don't know what *they*'ve drummed into his head. He's convinced he's on the right side."

Lyès-the-craftsman rolled a cigarette, tapped it on his knee and lit it with a lighter. The smoke hung in the air, unable to rise to the ceiling because of the heat. He stood and began pacing back and forth between the door and the window, his thoughts elsewhere. They had been talking in the public letter-writer's house for two hours, and he was beginning to get a headache.

"Boudema has always been a bit of a weathercock," said

Mourad, vexed. "He'd change direction with the slightest breeze. Since he joined the guerrillas, my father won't show his face outdoors any more."

"You still have a tiny bit of influence over him."

"Not any more. The police are looking for him . . ."

"I just don't understand anything any more," cried Lyès angrily. "Can someone tell me what's going on? If this is religion, then I don't want any of it. If the *Jihad* allows the slitting of a baby's throat, I'm not buying it. Each night, I tell myself: 'You'll see, it's a bad dream. Tomorrow you'll wake up.' And in the morning, I haven't finished rubbing my eyes when already a neighbour's been murdered. Shit! I want to understand what's going on."

"Understand what?" asked Dactylo. "It's perfectly obvious."

"What's obvious? The mists of time, barbarism, this crazy, stinking war? Why are the imams turning a deaf ear? Why is nobody doing anything? It's not by turning your back on disaster that you're going to stop it. Is that what religion's about?"

"It's got nothing to do with religion," said Dactylo. "That's a distraction, and has been since the beginning. The problem is elsewhere. They've taken the country and split it down the middle, just like that, at random. To some people they've said 'those are the *taghout*', and to others, 'these are the terrorists', and then they've sat back and watched the two tear each other apart."

"But why?"

"So as to have a free hand. There's big money at stake, large fortunes, investments . . ."

They suddenly stopped talking. A shadow had just moved on the patio.

"It's only me," yelped Zane appearing in the doorway.

"You knock first," said Dactylo, ill at ease.

"The door was open."

"It was closed."

"I'm telling you it was open. I'm no ghost, I can't walk through walls."

The three men stared at the dwarf muffled up in a grotesque *kamis*.

"What do you want?"

"I was passing by. I hope I'm not disturbing you."

"Don't be silly, of course not," said Mourad.

Zane extricated a bottle of Ricard, brandishing it triumphantly:

"I haven't come empty-handed."

"It's the first time you've managed to hide something," said Lyès sarcastically, "Normally you're the one hiding."

"That shows I'm beginning to be somebody."

Mourad grabbed the bottle and quickly filled the glasses sitting on the table amid the dirty plates and cigarette butts.

"I thought you'd chosen your side," went on Lyès suspiciously.

Zane let out a sigh like a schoolteacher unable to din the lesson into his pupil:

"Hey! These are terrible times. Everybody's talking about God and nobody knows which god they're talking about."

"We don't see you around in the evenings any more," pursued Lyès. "Can't you find your way in the dark?"

The craftsman's questions were beginning to irritate him, but Zane retained his composure. He said:

"Dwarves aren't hermaphrodites."

"Do you mean you're sleeping with someone?"

"This is a free country."

"A female dwarf?"

"A beefy widow with tits that could supply all the dairies in the Oran region."

"How do you mount her?"

"Sometimes I climb on a stool the way you taught me, sometimes she gets on top of me."

"And you manage to tickle her?"

"Well, you see, what I lack vertically, I make up for horizontally."

"True, you've got big feet."

Zane's face turned purple. His cheeks began to twitch uncontrollably. He stood staring into Lyès' eyes for a long time, then said icily:

"Lyès, my friend, it's unbelievable how careless you are."

Dactylo did not touch his glass, signalling to the intruder that he was not welcome. He sank into his upholstered chair, pressed his hands together against his nose and refused to pay the dwarf any attention. Outside, a donkey started braying.

Lyès pushed his glass away too:

"Perhaps it's poisoned."

Zane looked the public letter-writer up and down, then Lyès, picked up his bottle muttering and walked out without looking back. Lyès had to cut across the fields to catch up with him on the river bank.

"I haven't finished with you, you bastard. What did you mean, earlier, about my being careless?"

Zane turned on his heel and climbed up the bank. Lyès grabbed his arm and pulled him roughly down.

"Explain yourself, you little runt."

"I have nothing to say to you. When you stop winding me up . . ."

"No, that's not it. I find you strange, lately. I'm sure you're not spending the night with any widow. Am I right? Tell me, am I right? And yet, more than anything else in the world I'd like to be wrong about you. Don't look away when I'm talking to you. Tell me you're not involved with what's going on in the village . . ."

"Hey!" the dwarf protested vigorously. "Watch what you say. Are you trying to label me or what? I have nothing to do with those murderers."

"That would be terrible, Zane, terrible. There's no difference between the person who points out the victim and the one who commits the murder. Watch out, little man. Don't let them lure you. People's lives are at stake. It's no light matter. Watch out."

The dwarf spun round, horrified, and smashed his bottle against a rock:

"What are you talking about? Do you think I'm stupid? I had friends among the dead, don't you know. I was as fond of them as Mourad, Boudjema and you."

"So tell me where you got all this money that you're spending like water."

"You're imagining things, Lyès."

"And what about the plots of land you bought from the carpenter?"

"Are you spying on me or what?"

"I'm watching over you."

"If I understand correctly, you don't think dwarves are entitled to have a roof over their heads, or get married and live like normal people . . ."

"What's happening to you isn't normal. You're always either in the café or the mosque, and your pockets are stuffed with money . . ."

"You're jealous of my good fortune, if you want my opinion."

"I'm intrigued by your good fortune."

Zane freed himself like a spring. He jabbed a finger in the craftsman's chest, his face chalky, his eyes dilated and his mouth drooling.

"Do you want to know how I spend my nights, Lyès-the-craftsman? Well I'll tell you: drugs! There, are you happy? I sell dope . . . Now fuck off. I'm big enough to lead my life as I see fit. And I don't have to ask permission from anyone."

So saying, he spat to one side and went back to the village.

That night, Lyès was kidnapped. His body was never found.

Part 4

Chapter twenty

Rabah, the elder brother of Belkacem the baker, was piling the last bundles into the pick-up truck. Each time he went back into the house, it took him a little longer to come out again. He lingered in one of the rooms, or in front of the lemon tree, and miserably grabbed a chair or a package and returned to the vehicle.

The neighbours watched in silence from the opposite pavement. Children gathered at the end of the alley, some squatting, others perched in battered trees.

Rabah mopped his brow with a corner of his turban. His arm was shaking. He gazed at the sky, the hill-top, the fields, but not once did he turn towards the people. His brother, the baker, had been murdered inside the mosque. He himself had miraculously escaped an attack. Now that they had pushed cowardice so far as to send him threatening letters, he had decided to leave and never to set foot again in the village where he had been born and grown old, which no longer felt like home.

Sporting a brand new suit, Zane-the-dwarf paraded up and down in front of the truck. He had purposely not removed the label from his sunglasses so as to prove their authenticity. For some time, he had been flaunting the badge of his success with impunity. He polished his leather shoes with a silk handkerchief and turned his foot towards the sun to make it gleam, then inserted his thumbs under his braces and casually twanged them.

"Have you had a good look round?" he shouted to Rabah, "You haven't forgotten anything. Can I take possession of *my* house now? My tailor advised me not to expose my suit to the light for too long, you know."

Rabah gazed at his ancestors' house one last time, at the trough in which he had bathed as a child, and turned towards the old-fashioned objects piled onto the truck. A tear welled up in his eye. He quickly wiped it away, clambered into the cab and asked the driver to start up the engine. The truck shuddered with a grating racket and nosed its way through the crowd, chased by a horde of squealing brats.

Zane vaguely waved in the direction of the dust, smiling from ear to ear.

"I must have the road tarmacked around here, otherwise the gravel will ruin my soles."

Confronted by the silence of the old men, he adjusted his tie and added caustically:

"I'm going to do the place up from top to bottom. I'll put carved stone on the façades, green tiles above the gate, an entry phone on the gate post, then, when someone rings, I won't have to come out. I'll ask who it is in the microphone and, if it's a friend, I'll press the button and the door will open automatically. Like in the homes of the city nabobs. I'll also put a wrought-iron lamp in the courtyard, a rotating spray in the garden, balustrades around the veranda . . ."

People withdrew, one after the other, sickened by the dwarf's smug effrontery. Hadji Menouar shuffled off, overwhelmed, his face purple with indignation.

"This *douar* is going to the dogs," he muttered. "That nonentity, Zane, a land-owner! I should have died a hundred years ago."

He crossed the empty square. A handful of peasant-farmers were hanging around the café, their cheeks resting on their fists, their eyes almost rolling skywards. As games had been strictly forbidden by the fundamentalists, the domino players were at a complete loss. From dawn until dusk, they yawned until their jaws ached, so disconcerted that they no longer even talked.

A car pulled up in front of Hadji Menouar. Issa Osmane stepped out, arrogant in his shimmering burnous. He brushed the front of his robe and ran his fingers under his turban.

"I was looking for you, Sy Menouar."

"Ah . . ."

"I heard you were ill."

"Just an old man's foible," confessed Hadji Menouar. "It's the only trick we have left to get our kids to take pity on us. Why were you looking for me?"

Issa Osmane looked about him.

"Not here. Come into my car."

Hadji Menouar hesitated in front of the door opened for him.

"It won't take long," urged the former factotum. "It's very important."

Reluctantly, the old man gave in. Issa Osmane drove to the edge of the village, along the river and towards the Xaviers' farm.

"Do you remember?" he exclaimed, "the Xaviers' farm used to be so big. Goodness! The parties they used to have there, the officers in their uniforms like young gods, the *caids*, like sultans, and the women, ah, the women! Pretty like you wouldn't believe. Do you remember the vineyards stretching endlessly across the valley, the rains that obeyed us to the letter, the harvests that surpassed even the most optimistic forecasts? Those were the good old days, Hadji. On your honour, wasn't it heaven?"

"I don't remember anything."

"It's true, the ungrateful have no memory. But I remember everything. The Xaviers left, and they took with them the soul of the valley, the work ethos, the solemnity of the festivals and the rains too. It's strange, even the rivers have dried up. They left us an empire, and we've turned it into a rubbish dump. And look what the most prestigious farm in the region has become: a ruin. And the orchards, wasteland. And the forests where we used to picnic, deadly jungles."

"What do you want of me, Issa?"

"I bought the farm when 'Smail Ich was in charge of the town hall. I have the firm intention of reviving it. I'm going to replant the vineyards . . ."

"So what do you want of me?"

Issa parked his car under a tree, unwound his turban and flung it onto the back seat. His eyes froze in his ovoid head:

"Maurice is in danger . . ."

Hadji Menouar laughed silently.

Issa insisted:

"It's the truth. My son Tej has done everything he can to spare him, only, this time, the orders have come from on high and he can't do anything."

"Wait, wait," the old man grew irritated, "what are you trying to tell me?"

"What planet are you on, Sy Menouar? Foreigners have been declared undesirables. Those who refuse to leave the country are eliminated."

Incredulous, Hadji Menouar peered at his companion, looking for an indication in the network of wrinkles distorting his features that it was a bad joke. Issa's face dismayed him.

"I'm not with you."

"Maurice is a foreigner."

"Since when, if you please? His grandfather was born here. His family lived in the valley well before a good many of us. What you're saying is absurd."

"Absurd maybe, but true. His name is on the black list."

"Have you checked? Are you sure it's his name, his true name, really his name?"

"I repeat that if he's still with us, it's thanks to my son. I decided to talk to you because you're his best friend. You must warn him and persuade him to leave as soon as possible."

"He'd never agree to leave."

"But he must."

"Where do you expect him to go?"

"To France."

"He doesn't know where it is any more."

"Then let him go to Oran, or somewhere where he isn't known. I'm willing to help him. No, I won't drop him. He treated me well and I won't ever forget that. Since I found out he was in danger, I haven't been able to sleep either night or day."

"Wait, wait, not so fast. I can't take this in. Nobody would dare touch Maurice. It's unthinkable. I don't believe you."

Issa banged the steering wheel:

"You don't have the right to dismiss things. If you care about the poor bastard, hurry up and save his skin. A lot of Algerians of foreign origin have been murdered. They didn't take things seriously either. They considered themselves true natives. Result: they didn't have time to prove it. Even Arabs and Africans have been killed. We are the most racist nation on earth. Mere tourists, people simply passing through, have found out to their cost."

"I refuse to believe you."

"You are free to believe me or not to believe me, but I beg you, not at someone else's expense. Maurice must get out of here. I know he's got enough money to settle somewhere else. That's why I'm offering to buy his house. I'll pay his asking price. But he must move fast."

"No," said Hadji Menouar, shaking his chin vigorously, "we're no more racist than anyone else."

"There's no point putting our heads in the sand, Sy

Menouar. The truth is there. Refusing to believe it won't change much, sadly! I'm appalled too, terrified . . .”

“Shut up! For God's sake, shut up!”

Hadji Menouar got out of the car and walked back to the village, gesticulating like one possessed.

Issa picked up his turban, wound it carefully around his head and gazed at himself in the driving mirror. Delighted with his reflection, he winked at it and said:

“You have no more heart than a scorpion, Issa-the-disgrace. I'm surprised this mirror doesn't crack at the sight of you.”

“He doesn't want to know,” announced Hadji Menouar with an aching heart.

An undercurrent of emotion stirred the Elders gathered in the courtyard. Disoriented, they exchanged questioning looks, thumping their hands. Other people waited in the street, under the blazing sun. They had been there since the morning, huddling in the receding shade afforded by the wall. Dactylo stood apart with Jafer, contemplating the disconsolate faces of these old men who had come more to lament their own fate than that of their friend.

“We must do something,” said Issa Osmane from the depths of his car.

“What?” they replied. “Kick him out of his house?”

“That would be better than doing nothing,” cut in Zane. “Sy Issa is absolutely right. Maurice is pigheaded, but if anything happened to him, the surrounding villages would hold us responsible.”

"Let me talk to him," offered Sidi Saim's son.

The group jostling around the entrance to the patio moved back respectfully to allow him through.

"You won't get anywhere with him," Hadji Menouar warned him. "Maurice has withdrawn into himself."

"I understand, but he'll listen to me."

Sidi Saim's son entered the dark room with the windows closed. Hadji Maurice was hunched up in his wicker chair facing the wall, sleeping the sleep of the just. Only his shoulders and the back of his neck were visible.

"It's his way of sulking," explained Hadji Menouar. "If he won't listen to me, he won't listen to anyone else."

"He's right to rebuff us. It's, it's . . ."

Sidi Saim's son could not find his words. He nodded and withdrew, outraged.

"What kind of world are we living in?" raged Dactylo. "How can we tolerate this?"

"Absolutely," added Zane, affecting revulsion. "How can we tolerate this. Our families and friends are being hacked to pieces, and we don't lift a finger. We are allowing a handful of thugs to impose their laws on us when all we need to do is frown and they'll clear off."

The Elders retracted their necks into their shoulders. Dactylo kicked a can and left, with Jafer at his heels.

"Suppose we hid him at your place," suggested Zane trotting behind them. "That'd pull the wool over the Islamists' eyes."

"Islamists my foot! They have no more morality than a pack of hyenas. We're not stupid. Maurice, a foreigner? Since when, eh? Since they've had their eye on his house . . ."

Zane abandoned his attempt to catch up with them. His features shone with an alarming smugness. He calmly waited until they disappeared around the corner and returned to the Elders, rubbing his hands.

The night was filled with chirring. Ghachimat was holding its breath. Ghachimat always held its breath when the street lights went out. It meant that someone was going to die. Behind the windows, hearts were pounding. Not a sound in the streets, not a shadow . . . Around one o'clock in the morning, two trucks appeared out of the forest, drove through the village, around the square and stopped, one opposite Tej Osmane's garage and the other lower down to keep a lookout. Doors slammed. Shadows dispersed down the alleyway and surrounded Hadji Maurice's house.

From the top of his minaret, the muezzin watched the scene, his throat dry. At the slamming of the doors, his legs buckled and he withdrew behind the tannoy, pointing his finger skywards in prayer.

Hadji Menouar appeared on his doorstep clutching a cosh.

"Go indoors," ordered a masked man, releasing the breech-block of his gun.

Hadji Menouar dropped the cosh with a dull thud, and it rolled across the steps; he recoiled before the gun and disappeared.

Yusef noticed that the door of patio number 24 wasn't locked. He pushed it cautiously, standing to one side. The little courtyard was empty. Two men marched in, their guns cocked. The bedrooms were empty. The old man's bed had not been slept in.

"He's gone, the bastard," yelped Zane surreptitiously picking up a watch lying on the bedside table and slipping it into his pocket.

"There's never been a bastard in this house," said a croaky voice behind them.

Hadji Maurice was there, hunched in his wicker chair, in the dark at the end of the patio. Zane struck a match to locate him. In the flickering light, his perspiring face was sinister. Yusef groped around for the switch and turned on the light in the courtyard. Hadji Maurice looked relaxed in his voluminous white robe. He was fanning himself feebly.

"He hasn't gone," exulted Zane.

Yusef brandished a sabre:

"Too bad for him."

Boudjema restrained his arm:

"A bullet in the back of the neck will do the job."

Yusef shoved him violently away.

"I give the orders here."

"This is my home," the old man reminded him. "And you are not welcome here."

"What do we care," retorted Zane. "Colonialism is over. Tough luck on those who don't know it."

Four men threw themselves on Hadji Maurice, knocking him and his chair to the ground. Boudjema went out into the street so as not to witness the slaughter.

"Take off his robe," chuckled Zane. "Slit his throat . . . I want to see him struggle like a fat old pig . . . Shit! Look at all that blood. He's not a beast, he's a tank . . ."

Boudjema leaned against the wall, shivering from head to foot, his gaze fluttering around the moon like a moth around a candle.

Chapter twenty-one

As a child, Tej Osmane often used to sit outside the garage where he would later learn the trade of mechanic. But not to learn about engines. Cupping his face in his hands, he preferred to contemplate the "villa" opposite. Sometimes, when someone went in or came out, the door opened wide enough to give him a glimpse of part of the garden, a blaze of brilliantly coloured flowers lovingly tended by the French schoolteacher. He didn't recall ever playing in a garden. At his place, in the filthy old shack where his family vegetated, there was just a ragged plot where his father grew potatoes and onions. Unable to sell them at the market, he had to eat some every day so as to be able to put a little money aside, just in case. Tej did not even allow himself to run around with the boys of his age in the orchards or the village square. Nobody wanted him. The others would often chase him away with sticks and obscenities. So he would come to forget his troubles opposite the patio of number 24. He thought that it was around that age that he had begun to dream of a garden just for him, where he would be able to escape from the cruelty and humiliation his pals inflicted on him. The "villa" had been built by Maurice's father. He had raised it, brick by brick, like a tomb. It was pretty, completely different from all the other houses in the village, with its façade inlaid with blue stones, its slate roof and elegant gables.

Now, his dream had come true. Hadji Maurice's house was his. *And only his.*

Standing on top of Djebel el-Khouf, Tej Osmane dominated the whole world. At his feet the valley displayed its offering of hills, rivers, orchards and fields, and its grey-tinged horizons. Tej was convinced that all he had to do was stretch out his hand to pluck them all at once. But it was neither Maurice's house nor the vista over the valley that made him look so radiant. Tej firmly believed that his patience was at last beginning to bear fruit: the regional command of the GIA had just made him an emir. He would rule single-handedly over the entire region.

Kada Hilal had been relieved of his duties. A zealous prose writer, more concerned with his turns of phrase than the reversal of military situations, the valiant "Afghan" proved as useless a warrior as he was a mediocre leader of men. In view of the ineffectiveness of his actions – denounced in an anonymous report – an emissary had been despatched to assess the crack in the *Jihad* operation. Kada welcomed him with exaggerated consideration, and bored him rigid with tedious discourses. During the emissary's stay, Tej refrained from saying a word to corroborate the criticisms in the report. One week later, Kada was relieved.

"I expect you've been promoted," Tej told him.

The megalomaniac "Afghan" believed him. He even promised to champion him before the Majlis.

Before taking leave, Kada liked to speak to his *Mujahedin* and kiss their heads as Sheikh Abbas had kissed his the day of his departure for Afghanistan.

"I can't let you leave like that," said Tej. "I made you a promise and I intend to keep it."

Kada agreed to stay with the *katiba* a few days longer. From morning to evening, in the shade of a tent, he gathered his flock and gave free rein to his fantasies.

Tej laughed long and hard over this burlesque prophet who was a mere pawn on the chessboard of his ambitions, doomed to the inevitable fate reserved for things that had outlived their usefulness.

"Look at you, smiling to yourself, Tej," said Yusef, catching him unawares.

"Emir Tej Ed-Dine!"

"Excuse me, Emir Tej Ed-Dine . . . Is the big day in sight?"

"We mustn't wait for the days to come, but we must go towards them, conquer them and tame them. It is men who make and unmake fate, men who bend History to their purpose."

He ran his hands through his long hair, and squinted as if to make out something in the distance. "Earlier, gazing at the valley, I had a vision."

"A happy one, I hope."

"I hate that word," snapped Tej, suddenly irritated. "What is hope? What does it mean, to hope?"

"I didn't mean anything, it just came out of my mouth."

"It's not good. You shouldn't just say anything 'that comes out of your mouth'. Especially when you're in the process of winning a challenge."

Yusef was somewhat nonplussed by the new emir's rise to prominence in the *katiba*. Was he taking charge? He looked sheepish and began fiddling with the safety catch on his gun. Tej quickly regained his composure. He smoothed his beard with a mystical gesture, allowed his gaze to sweep over the valley again and said in a conciliatory tone:

"To hope means to wait for a miracle to happen, Yusef. And miracles have to be made to happen. Someone who really *wants* to get there can't wait. Time doesn't wait. It only grants its favours to the tireless runners. In the marathon imposed on us by the *taghout* – since this is a war of attrition – each stride we take must be negotiated with the utmost rigour and calculation. We must leave nothing to chance. If chance is on our side, there's no guarantee that it will continue to be so. Chance is only with the tireless runners. That's why they succeed in turning the tables, in catching the world off-guard. It's true that one sometimes needs a helping hand from fate. But fate only assists visionary opportunists. Chance is a comet which we must, if not track down, at least intercept. If it passes us by, we lose face for eternity."

"We've already grabbed its tail. The country is on its knees. All we have to do now is deal the final blow. Do you think our sword is long enough to stab its heart?"

"Do you doubt it?"

"So what are we waiting for?"

"We're not waiting. We draw our inspiration from its dying gasps. It's not a matter of finishing it off, Yusef, but of punishing it, dragging it through the mud so as better to subjugate it. The best slave is the one you conquer. The slave you buy or who is given to you is not trustworthy; a part of him will always question your authority over him."

He clenched his fist, shook it and brandished it in the face of the world:

"It's all in there, Yusef. The whole secret of the universe is contained in this fist. If one little finger slackens, the entire world eludes our grasp."

Despite the late hour, Ghachimat had not extinguished all its lights. The sound of children making a commotion in the houses and the clanging of kitchen utensils could be heard. There was a full moon, illuminating the recesses of the door-ways. A pack of dogs was rummaging about in the refuse heaps piled up in the deserted streets. Some of the beasts suddenly stopped sniffing the rubbish, pricked up their ears and then, one after the other, they beat a retreat towards the river, and were soon overtaken by two tractors and a pick-up crammed with ragged, bearded figures.

Roused by the throbbing of the engines, shadows appeared at the windows and hurriedly secured the shutters. In a trice, the village was shrouded in darkness.

The three vehicles entered the village square. Tej Osmane stepped out, signalling to his men to disperse around him. Some fifty terrorists, armed with guns and sabres, divided into two groups. The first made its way towards the mayor's house, Tej at their head. The second, commanded by Yusef, silently surrounded the mosque and marched on the Sidhoms' house, where Zane, perched on a rock, surveyed the area like a bird of prey on the lookout.

Allal's mother was finishing her prayers. Kneeling on the mat, she muttered some verses. Her two daughters were chatting in a corner, leafing through an old magazine.

"Someone's at the door," said one.

The other looked at the alarm-clock on the chest of drawers.

"Who can that be?"

The mother stood up, rolled up the mat and put it on the upholstered seat.

"I'll go and see."

"No," said the girl anxiously.

"In any case, if they want to harm us, I don't see how we can stop them. They'll just knock the door down."

The mother went out into the courtyard.

"Who's there?"

"Zane, Aunt Ayesha. Allal's sent you some money."

"Slip it under the door."

"I can't. There's also a parcel for you."

The two girls joined their mother on the patio. Ashen-faced, they stood with their arms around each other's waists. The mother hesitated, then drew back the bolt. Zane smiled before showing her his empty palms.

"Got you, old lady! I don't have anything for you. But my friends do."

Yusef shoved him aside, grabbed the old woman by her

hair and flung her to the ground. Before it dawned on her what was happening, he brandished his sabre and decapitated her.

On the other side of the village, a tractor reversed into the door of the mayor's residence and smashed it down. It was greeted by shots fired from the first floor. An attacker was hit. He collapsed with an expletive. The sten-guns rattled out their fire in the direction of the window, shattering the panes to smithereens. The tractor destroyed the garden then rammed the front door. Tej clambered over a low wall to reach the back of the house, and threw a hand-made grenade into the room. A fountain of flames and dust spurted out of the sky-light. About ten terrorists took advantage to climb onto the terrace, blow out a French window and disappear into the house. Bursts of gunfire rang out, amid the screams of the women and children, then the mayor collapsed, wounded in the shoulder and legs. He tried to crawl towards his gun. 'Smail Ich stopped him by crushing his neck under his foot.

"That's the end of your heroism, you son-of-a-bitch. You've had your go. It's our turn now."

The terrorists rushed down to the ground floor where the women and children were gathered. The mayor's blind mother was trying to calm her family, her arms outstretched in the void. Tej casually shot her in the head, without even looking at her. The old woman crumpled like a curtain, spattering the floor with her blood. Sarah tried to protect her little brothers by hugging them to her. Tej seized her by the throat and marched her out into the courtyard.

"Look at your family," said 'Smail to the dying mayor. "They say there's nothing worse than outliving your children.

Well, tonight, you're going to discover something even better. You're going to witness their deaths. We're going to slit their throats in front of your eyes, one after the other, then we'll sodomize your wife, gouge out her eyes, rip off her fingers and the skin from her back, cut off her breasts and then we'll slice her to pieces with a hacksaw. And when we've finished with your family, I'll personally douse your body in petrol and take great delight in burning you. You wanted to play with fire. I bring you the fires of hell."

And he threw his head back in a terrible laugh.

Yusef and his group withdrew from the Sidhoms' house and joined Tej's men around the mayor's residence. Zane waited until they had disappeared behind the mosque before returning to the blood-drenched patio. He stepped over the dismembered body of old Ayesha, knelt before the corpses of the two girls, rolled up the dress of one of them and began unzipping his trousers.

Chapter twenty-two

Never had the Ghachimat cemetery been so busy since the start of the hostilities. An unexpectedly large crowd insisted on accompanying the victims to their final resting place. People had come from all around, from Moulay Naim to the most remote little villages in the region, their mouths set in anger and disgust. The administrative authorities surrounded Allal Sidhom, who stood ashen-faced but dignified. The eleven bodies lay in a row in front of their graves, covered in flags. It had taken all the able-bodied men to recover the eight charred bodies of the mayor's family from the ruins: one man, two women and five children, including two infants. A surgeon from the town had been despatched to the Sidhoms' house to reassemble the mutilated bodies of the mother and her two daughters.

The imam of Moulay Naim addressed the dismayed crowd:

"Can anyone tell me why these poor creatures were brutally murdered? I'll tell you why: because we were unable to protect them. As a result, we are as guilty as their murderers. We are about to consign their remains to the earth, but their spirit will live on in ours. We are unworthy to survive them. We chose the most dishonourable attitude. We are saddened at the tragedy in the morning, but we hurry to wash our hands of it by evening. And one night, it will be our turn. Only then will we understand why a small band of dogs is terrorizing an entire nation, why, every day, children, women, the elderly, the infirm, infants must die, and why other children and women, other survivors must give them a mean and shameful burial."

After the funeral, Allal withdrew with Jafer. They stood on a mound of earth watching the crowd disperse and the cars drive off amid clouds of dust. The Elders lingered in the graveyard, their faces tinged with purple, their cheeks quivering with rage and helplessness. At the foot of the hill, the heat shimmered like a swamp. Allal crouched down then sat on the mound, took his head in both hands and let out a howl that neither the mountain nor the vastness seemed big enough to contain.

Zane and a group of volunteers were swabbing down the Sidhoms' patio. Bloody rivulets ran into the street. With a huge broom, the dwarf set about scrubbing the clotted stains that had dried on the flagstones. On hearing Allal arrive, he stopped scraping and shouted:

"In any case, they won't make it into Paradise. One

day, we'll catch them and we'll make them pay for their barbarism. Attacking poor old Ayesha. How low can you get? Such a discreet, vulnerable old woman . . ."

He pretended he had just noticed Allal standing behind him:

"I'm sorry, I can't help it. No man in his right mind can accept such depravity. Your mother was a saint. She was fond of me."

Allal made a gesture of thanks and went to join his friends inside the house.

"It's our fault," exploded Mourad. "In other villages people are getting organized and demanding weapons to defend themselves, but we're just sitting here being smug. Because most of the terrorists in the region are from here, we think they're going to spare us. And this is the result. And it's not over. They'll be back to massacre other neighbours, other cousins, other poor bastards."

"Too right," agreed Houari, a small, skinny man who had lost two fingers in a joiner's workshop. "Those sons-of-bitches are afraid of nothing."

"They've murdered babies . . ."

"They've killed their inner God. The only thing that drives them is the blood running in our veins. They'd even attack ink-wells to empty them of their ink."

"Let's keep to the point, please," said Mourad. "The question is: when are we going to set up our own self-defence group?"

A devastating silence settled over the room. Eyes looked

away, heads bowed, hands strayed over knees. Someone rose and pretended to close the window. Someone else offered to clear the tables. Mourad caught him by the shoulder and forced him to look him in the eye:

"There's no rush, Tahar. Leave the plates and glasses where there are. They're not about to explode in our faces."

Tahar was embarrassed. He suffered the grip on his shoulder with suppressed anger.

Mourad turned to the others.

"What's the matter with you lot? Have I said something wrong or have you lost your tongues?"

He scornfully pushed Tahar against the wall. With his finger, he drew an accusing arc.

"You shit your pants as soon as we talk about serious issues. Well let me tell you: you're less than dirt, cowards, nothing but cowardly hypocrites and wretches."

"That's not it," a young builder protested feebly.

"So what is it, then?"

"There are informers everywhere, Mourad. Don't imagine that the person who smiles at you is on your side. Ghachimat is crawling with vipers."

"You're right," agreed Zane vehemently. "We're not cowards. We don't trust anyone, that's all."

Mourad thumped the ground with his fist.

"Too easy to wriggle out of it. But not any more. We have no choice. Either we take up arms against these thugs or it's every man for himself. If there are informers – and indeed there are – we all know who they are. We simply have to turn them over to the police. Let's rid our village of rats. Track the bastards down. Let's protect our families and our possessions, our friends and our dignity. Many of you agree with me, think as I do and are ready to do battle. It's the failure to communicate that isolates us. So let's break the wall of silence. Let's put our cards on the table. At Moulay Naim, there are twelve of us with shotguns. We've agreed to set up our own self-defence group. If there are any volunteers from Ghachimat, now's the time to join us. Right away. Rahal-the-penitent has agreed to give us a hand. He has experience, knows the terrain and I trust him completely."

Once again, the men's shoulders and necks bowed under the torture of silence. After lengthy consideration, Zane cried:

"I volunteer."

His enthusiasm did not relax the atmosphere. All eyes turned to Allal, and away again. Houari coughed into his fist to clear a big clot in his throat. He said:

"I have two old guns at home."

"Keep one for me," said his neighbour morosely.

"I'm with you, Mourad," shouted an old man in the doorway.

One by one, hands were raised with varying degrees of conviction. Mourad began to count them, and to ask those who were still undecided to make up their minds.

"Twelve! That's twenty-four altogether. It's not bad, and I congratulate you. Let's strike while the iron's hot and meet this evening to discuss how to put our self-defence unit into operation. I've already spoken to the military commander of Zitoune. He'll arm us better and give us the help we need. We're no longer alone, friends. We'll rid our villages of the blight of fundamentalism, I promise you."

In the room, suddenly, the coolness of evening caused shudders down the spine.

Mother Osmane wearily adjusted her headscarf. At sixty-four, she was no more than a wreck, with a creased face and a dying look in her eyes. The wife of Issa-the-disgrace, she had shared his humiliations and suffering with a rare forbearance. Whereas the factotum had willingly grovelled to others, she had borne her family's disappointments with astonishing resoluteness. Poverty and debasement had never broken her spirit. A common skivvy, exploited and scorned by the entire village, a ghost trailing herself and her antecedents through the hostile streets of Ghachimat, she only had to step over the threshold to become a different personality and the mistress of her home. She ruled over her children with a ruthless authority. Her orders flew like summons, and her decisions were final. Nobody argued with her in the home. Even Tej obeyed her absolutely and worshipped her. The women who took unfair advantage of her and paid a few miserable dinars loathed her. They found she had a kind of dignity that remained intact regardless of their contempt, and they were wary of her opaque, disturbing stoicism, like still water. Mother Osmane submitted without ever giving the impression of humbling herself, absorbed insults as blotting paper soaks up ink, and when someone tried to humiliate her, she would meet her attacker's gaze and force even the most disdainful eyes to look away. This especially was why they hated her. Mother Osmane belonged to that race of victims who, even relegated to the very lowest rungs of society, constantly rise to the top to haunt people. Just like the viper she was always compared to, she inspired repugnance and fear in equal measures.

"Why aren't you eating?" she asked Issa, who lay prostrate in front of his plate.

"Why do you think?"

Mother Osmane sat silently on a stool, facing her husband. Her blank expression flitted around the room before her eyes met Issa's.

"I'm tired."

"Go to bed."

"Hurry up and finish your supper so I can clear the table."

"I'm not hungry."

"You haven't eaten anything all day."

Issa was exasperated by his wife's toneless voice. His jaws worked up and down in his disconcerted face, and he clenched his fists.

"Tej shouldn't have attacked the village like that," he said.

"Why?"

"Now we've got everyone on our backs."

"Stand up and shake them off."

Issa thought he discerned scorn in his wife's fixed smile.

"You really must be very tired."

"Of seeing you in that state."

"What do you expect me to do? Rejoice? Go out and celebrate my son's brilliant leadership?"

"Tej knows what he's doing."

"Oh yes . . ."

The mother joined her two hands in the fold of her

dress. For a fleeting moment, her face burned with an un-pleasant, enigmatic expression.

"Absolutely."

"It was a bad idea. Attacking Ghachimat, where his parents live, is sheer idiocy. It's as if he were offering us for a lynching. I can't even go out on my own patio."

"Nothing will happen to us. Our son is powerful. He's the regional emir and his arm is so long that he can strike where and when he wants. People know that. Otherwise they'd have murdered us before even going to the cemetery to bury the mayor and that low-class family of his."

Issa was not convinced. He wearily nodded his head.

"No, not Ghachimat. It was pointless, crazy . . ."

"I asked him to do it."

Issa looked sharply up at his wife, his eyebrows bristling: "What?"

"You heard."

Issa was completely at a loss. He was so overwhelmed, it took a few moments for her words to sink in. His strained face turned ashen and the dark shadows around his eyes were accentuated. For a minute, he gulped, his throat dry and his breath coming in gasps.

"It isn't possible," he panted. "You can't do that to us. I refuse to believe you."

"I haven't asked anything of you."

His wife's toneless voice made his blood run cold. He made a feeble gesture, as if to brush away a fly, but his com-panion's lifeless gaze left no room for doubt.

"You?"

"They were all useless," she muttered. "They didn't

deserve to live. They didn't know the meaning of the word."

"What are you talking about, you crazy old woman?"

"They thought they were the masters. They disposed of the wretched as they saw fit. They had no more regard for the poor than they had self-respect. All they did was steal, cheat and despise. The more they had, the more they wanted. Their greed and self-importance were boundless. They made me suffer, those bastards. I haven't forgotten a single incident, not one thing. I haven't forgiven a single one of them, either. It's all etched here," she added in a flat voice, jabbing her temple. "But never, ever did I despair. I raised Tej solely to avenge me. And I'm going to enjoy it."

Issa pushed away the table and rose. His wife's iciness created in him a mixture of terrible panic and horror.

"Let me remind you that children were murdered."

"Mine weren't so lucky. They died every day, on every street corner. Wherever they set foot, they were persecuted, hounded out, humiliated, mauled, then they were revived to be handed over to the torturers once again. You cannot understand, Issa. You soon laid down your arms. You felt that the wrongs they made you suffer were legitimate. And you couldn't see much because you insisted on keeping your head down and your eyes on the ground. But I didn't lay down my arms. I hid them away until now. If you wound a beast, you must finish it off. They didn't do that. That's their lookout . . ."

She too rose. Slowly, Issa grasped her shoulders, crushing her against the wall, beside himself:

"You're completely mad."

"You're hurting me."

Issa sat down again. He shook his head several times:

"I refuse to believe you."

"I don't care."

Once again, Issa laid his hands on his wife. This time, his fingers didn't reach her shoulders. They remained frozen in mid-air, like petrified talons. Mother Osmane pushed him away, picked up the tray and went back into the kitchen. Issa gazed after her incredulously, at a total loss, and collapsed on an upholstered seat.

"It's not the end of the world," rasped a voice.

Issa turned round. Zane-the-dwarf was standing in the doorway, staring at him menacingly.

"How did you get in?"

Offended, Zane pouted.

"Everyone asks me the same question: how did you get in? As if there were any secret. I don't walk through walls. I knocked, turned the handle and came in. That's what everyone else does, isn't it?"

Issa looked at the alarm-clock on the television set, and realized that he had dozed off for a few minutes. He rubbed the nape of his neck and looked at the dwarf.

"What do you want? It's almost ten o'clock at night, and I'm sleepy."

"Precisely. I've come to wake you up. No question of getting any sleep tonight, my friend. I've just come back from Moulay Naim where I attended a terrible meeting. Mourad and Allal are setting up a self-defence group. They'll be the talk of the town tomorrow. They've decided to go and get Sarah. They're armed and they're determined."

"How many of them are there?"

"Twenty-two."

"Tej will make mincemeat of them."

"Maybe, but it's started. Soon all the youngsters will follow their example and, in less than a week, we'll have a contingent of 'patriots' on our hands. They're already drawing up lists to ask for guns. I saw with my own eyes a representative from the army give them the forms to register. They're also talking about the possibility of stationing a local guard around here. I'm not telling you this to push you, but if I were in your shoes, I'd start getting my suitcases down from the attic straight away."

Issa contemplated the ceiling, trying to muster his thoughts. Zane took advantage to rush over to the upholstered seat, and settle himself comfortably between two cushions, crossing his legs.

"There's something else . . . People aren't at all happy. I hung around the café. I assure you my ears are still buzzing. Tej has made a big mistake. While he was terrorizing other parts, nobody was bothered. But he shouldn't have attacked Ghachimat . . ."

"Get to the point."

"OK," said Zane. "I'll be blunt: they're out to get you!"

Issa curled his lip in an indecisive grin.

"Well, well . . ."

"At the café you only hear one word: revenge. Everybody's got to have their say. Some are for slitting your throat, others for burning, but they all agree on one thing: wiping you out, you and your whole family. I assure you they're very determined. I wouldn't be surprised if, in less than an hour, your house . . ."

"Let them come then," said Issa becoming irritated. "What are they waiting for? An invitation from me?"

"There's no point getting all het up. Get a move on and pack your bags, and get out of here, fast. In Ghachimat and Moulay Naim, all people can think of is hacking you to bits. Even your friend Adda wants to hang you at the entrance to the village. And Boudaoura says he'll plait the rope himself. The wind has turned, Issa my friend."

"Whose side are you one, you evil gnome? The way you talk, you sound thrilled."

"I took a huge risk in coming to warn you. Isn't that enough? I'm sure they've sent at least three or four men here to watch you, or even to crucify you. And that didn't stop me coming to see you. What further proof of my loyalty do you need? I've never let down my friends."

"That's a likely story, Zane. Don't you think you can get round me. We are of the same ilk: there's no exceptional courage in our blood. Tell me exactly what it is you're after, and let's get it over with."

Zane faked outrage. He leapt up, but not violently enough to intimidate Issa.

"Just hurry up and get out of here."

And, pretending to be very upset, he left.

Zane did not go home that night. He hid behind a clump of cacti, keeping his eyes glued to Hadji Maurice's former house. He soon heard the Osmanes moving around. Leaving nothing to chance, Zane climbed a tree overlooking the patio. He saw Issa's children coming and going in the courtyard, carrying bundles and packages, piling their load into a pick-up in a state of frenzied but muffled agitation.

Not a cry, not a sound. Once the truck was full, Issa came out carrying two small suitcases. He placed one on the steps and the other in the cab of the truck. Then he sent his youngest son to fetch Attou-the-refuse-collector.

For most people, Attou was an insignificant, harmless old man, a poor soul as lost as the shadow he dragged behind him all day long. He wasn't despised – people were barely aware of his existence. But in fact, since the advent of fundamentalism, Attou had discovered a vocation. It was his job to hand over the funds collected by sympathizers and the money extracted from citizens by force to the local armed groups.

Thanks to his discretion and his status of a pariah, he could go to the clandestine hideouts at all hours without arousing suspicion.

Zane returned to his look-out post behind the cacti. Attou arrived a few moments later, still sleepy, his hair tousled.

"Here's the money for Tej," Issa told him. "Find a way of getting it to him before the end of the week. Tell him we've left for Louisa's. He'll understand."

"Are you leaving?"

"We've got good reason not to hang around here any longer."

Attou wiped his nose on a corner of his robe. He realized that in his hurry he had left his glasses at home. But what worried him more was the sudden departure of his allies. He stared at the truck piled with baggage and passengers, the empty house, the suitcase at his feet.

"You have nothing to worry about," Issa reassured him. "Nobody knows about you and me."

Attou didn't dwell on the subject. He picked up the suitcase and made to leave. Issa restrained his arm:

"You're a good person, Attou. Tej thinks very highly of you."

"A fat lot of good that does me."

"We won't abandon you, I promise. As soon as I'm settled in, I'll send someone to fetch you."

Attou stared at his feet, wriggled his toes around the thong of his sandals and said indifferently:

"Huh! You know, at my age . . ."

"Take care of yourself."

Attou looked up, intrigued by Issa's emotion, found it hard to believe, turned on his heel and left, dragging his feet lazily.

"Right," said Issa to his family, crammed into the truck, "let's push off."

The truck revved up and drove off the patio, its lights extinguished. Avoiding the main street, it headed through the village, bumping over the tracks around the outskirts. The brake lights went on at every pot-hole. Eventually it reached the tarmacked road at the foot of the hill, and immediately disappeared into the night.

Attou waited for it to vanish before spitting venomously over his shoulder and stamping his foot on the ground.

"*We won't abandon you*," he grumbled. "Time will tell. Bastards! I curse you!"

He concealed the suitcase under his arm and hurried back to his hovel. He walked past the mayor's burnt-out home, turned back because of a gang of youths chatting over a late-night coffee, went up narrow, unlit streets, stopping from time to time to make sure nobody was following him. Suddenly, a familiar, nimble shadow leapt out of a prickly pear hedge and intercepted him. Attou just had time to glimpse a reflection on the blade of the knife. A searing pain ripped through his guts. He dropped the suitcase to clutch his stomach with both hands, and slowly fell to his knees. For a fraction of a second, the shadow stepped into the moonlight. Attou recognized Zane's grimacing face. Once again, the knife whistled through the air and came down to slit his throat from ear to ear. Felled, Attou caught sight of the warm blood running between his fingers. He keeled forwards, face down on the ground, and did not move again.

Zane turned the old man's decapitated body over gingerly, with the toe of his shoe, and felt it. Satisfied, he wiped the bloodstained blade on the dead man's robe, grabbed the suitcase and vanished into the night like an evil spirit.

Attou's body was discovered early the next morning, lying in a pool of blood. To the crowd that had gathered around the body, Zane said:

"It's begun! The hour of vengeance has struck. Woe to the 'rats', for the 'patriots' will have no mercy on them."

And at the café, all day long:

"Can you believe it? Attou, a rat?"

"Attou? That loser, an informer?"

Chapter twenty-three

"From now on, we're in hostile territory," said Rahal-the-penitent. "Nothing must be left to chance. The terrorists could be anywhere, and the paths are likely to be littered with explosive devices. Don't pick anything up, don't rush and watch where you step."

He shifted his gun to his shoulder to crouch down, and asked the group to gather around him. He drew circles on the ground with a stick.

"This is more or less how the land lies. Here's the north. This circle here is the mountain just to our left. We are roughly here, on its south-east flank."

He drew a winding line through the circles and added:

"This is our path. We'll walk in single file. You see the woods at the foot of the hill. There's a stream. The terrorists had a training camp there which the army finally discovered.

From time to time, helicopters bombard it. The mob that hung out there must have retreated much further south. Tej's camp has to be around here somewhere, behind the forest. There are probably advance observation posts not far from where we are now. From now on, our group will split into three teams. Bouhafs, Hashem and I will go ahead and scout around. Baroudi, Hamida and Fodil will stay behind and cover us. The others will be in the middle. There must be no more than three hundred metres between teams. You mustn't take your eyes off the person in front. In the event of a hitch, keep calm. If we are shot at, we throw ourselves to the ground and seek cover immediately. Don't, under any circumstances, shoot back blindly. Firstly, to save on ammunition, and secondly so as not to give those sons-of-bitches any idea of our number. So, only shoot when the target is in the line of sight. Don't leave your hiding place other than for one that is better protected, and get someone else to cover you."

He stood up.

"Any questions?"

The group exchanged glances. Around him, the grey mountains seemed to tower a fraction higher. Not a cloud had ventured forth. The birds were singing at the tops of their voices, leaves rustled; but the murmur of the woods was unable to soothe the dull thudding in the men's temples. Someone wiped his arm over his dripping brow, and turned around as if to gauge the universe that separated him from his village. He could make out only a far-off splatter of light, as frightening as a precipice.

Rahal sensed the disquiet that was spreading through the group. He unhooked his gun, grasped it firmly and said:

"If anyone has second thoughts, now's the time for them to go back home. This isn't a stroll in the country, I'm warning you. It's unlikely we'll come out unscathed."

"Advance," ordered Mourad, exasperated. "We're not softies."

Rahal nodded. After a last glance at his companions, he spun round and set off among the thickets, Bouhafs and Fodil at his heels.

Mourad, Allal, Jafer and seven other volunteers waited a few minutes before setting off, leaving behind the team whose job was to cover the rear.

At around three o'clock in the afternoon, they reached a clearing and decided to halt for a while. During the advance, they had not come across anything suspicious, not the slightest sign of life. They felt as though they were in limbo. The few shacks they did encounter had been abandoned months earlier. Some had been burned down, others completely demolished, they looked like something out of a nightmare. Even the streams had been buried under piles of stones. The territory was devastated, as if a curse had befallen it. There was a farm high up in the forest where people used to breed livestock and make cheese. Now it was nothing but a gloomy ruin, marking the point of no-return. The walls had caved in, the roofs blown off; there were no doors left standing, or windows. Only blackened patches marked the positions of enclosures destroyed by the barbarous advance of the fundamentalists.

"It's utter destruction," commented Houari.

Mourad sat on a dead tree trunk and began removing his espadrilles. He took off his socks, wrung them out and laid them on a burning hot rock. His feet were bleeding and

179

blistered. He wiped around his ankles and between his toes with a cloth. He was so infuriated that he paid no attention to his companion.

Allal and Jafer went to rest in the shade of a conifer. They opened their bags in silence and pulled out their lunch protected by wrapping paper. The policeman contemplated his portion wearily, and put it down beside him.

"You need to keep your strength up," advised Jafer.

Allal merely acquiesced, but made no effort to pick up his sandwich. Since the murder of his family, he had lived in a sort of trance. He no longer spoke, ate very rarely and, at night, he never switched off the light in his bedroom. Sometimes, when he shut himself away to commune with his departed, his face grew dark, his entire body went rigid and he had a cataleptic fit that lasted for hours, leaving people wondering whether he would ever come out of it.

"I was very impressed with Rahal," said Jafer in the hope of stimulating his friend. "He seems a seasoned fighter. I find his confidence reassuring."

"It's natural," broke in Tahar. "He was in Afghanistan and operated with the most feared terrorists in the region for two years. He knows this area like the back of his hand. But a penitent remains a penitent. When someone's betrayed once, they're a traitor for life."

Jafer was disconcerted by this last remark. He wheeled round to face Tahar:

"What does that mean?"

Tahar shrugged:

"That's my personal opinion. I don't trust the fellow. We have no proof that he's not taking us for a ride."

Jafer frowned.

"Mourad says we can rely on him."

"Mourad's a junkie. He lost his judgement ages ago. Rahal has repented, for certain, but not for moral reasons, even less out of conviction. He fell foul of his emir and he was in danger of being executed by his peers. That's what was behind his surrender. He's a bastard like the others. He's murdered loads of poor bastards, and I'm sure he doesn't regret it one little bit. He's a killer, you mark my words. I can't get a wink of sleep with a fellow like that next to me."

"Why did you follow him?"

"I didn't follow him. Allal is my friend. I'm helping him look for Sarah. That said, I think it would be a good idea to keep a close watch on Rahal. In any case, I'm keeping my wits about me. If I detect the slightest irregularity, I won't give him the time to cover up."

"You're talking nonsense."

"Maybe, but I don't want to die any old how. I'm absolutely convinced that someone who has betrayed once is a traitor for life. Perhaps that's too harsh, but it's pointless ignoring it."

So saying, Tahar rolled up his jacket, wedged it against a rock and lay down his head to sleep for a moment. Jafer continued to gaze at him for a few minutes. He picked up his sandwich and realized he had lost his appetite.

At dawn on the second day, the group reached scrubland scorched by old artillery fire. In the midst of the charred bushes and blackened craters, just at the end of a track streaked with ruts, three human heads were decomposing in the sun. They had been slit at the throat, and were swaying on the end of branch. The place was contaminated by the stench of the gruesome trophies, and Mourad and his companions stood in stunned shock at the sight. Some of them clapped their hands over their mouths and turned away, others felt their knees go weak. Someone bent double and began vomiting with loud groans.

"Welcome to Amazonia," said Rahal.

"Why Amazonia?" stammered Mourad. "The real cannibals were born here."

Further on, they discovered a nomad's tent, recognizable by its crudely patched fabric and spindly supports. Two decapitated women lay beside an overturned cooking pot. Inside the shack lay the disembowelled body of a baby, rotting in its cradle, covered in a swarm of voracious flies.

"Shit! Look at that!"

"What can they have done to deserve to die like that?"

"That's just it, they haven't done anything."

"Hey!" shouted Rahal at the foot of a mound. "There are more bodies over here."

Five men, three of whom had been decapitated, were lying in the midst of a meagre herd of goats that had been decimated. They were naked, and their flesh showed deep scars from being tortured. Lying beside each other, a little boy and a little girl held hands. They looked as though they were dreaming. If only their slender necks had not been defiled by the blade of a sabre or machete . . .

"Let's move," said Rahal, running agilely down the hill.

The sun was having difficulty rising over the mountain.

In the silence of the woods, the buzzing of the flies vied with the stench of decomposing bodies. For Mourad and his men, even if hell was worse than all the horrors of the earth, it alone could not diminish them.

The first terrorist look-out post was only spotted later in the afternoon. It took all Rahal's experience and skill to discover it, camouflaged behind some bushes and inaccessible. It covered a hilltop and dominated the only route to that part of the mountain, hemmed in by uneven terrain. Rahal scrutinized the hillside with his binoculars, lingering patiently over the bushes, on the alert.

"There are two of them," he announced. "I can get them."

He signalled to Mourad's team not to move, then, crawling through the tangled grass, he nimbly ascended the bank. A few interminable minutes later, a shot rang out, followed by a short burst of fire and a cry. Bouhafs and Fodil immediately ran towards the river, to take the target from the rear. A shotgun rang out, followed close by two other bursts of gunfire.

"What's going on?" yelled the rear guard running towards Mourad's team.

"Get back to your posts," shouted Jafer with a note of uncertainty. "We've spotted two terrorists."

Three shots rasped out on top of the ridge. Bouhafs and Fodil attacked the post, inspected the surrounding area and came back and showed themselves on top of the hill, signalling to the rest of the group to join them. Mourad went first, cursing the breech of his gun which was jammed, and began to career like a madman through the bushes. On the mound, a ragged terrorist lay with his arms outstretched, his beard down to his navel and his head blown off by gunfire.

"The other one ran off that way," said Fodil, feverishly. "Rahal was hot on his heels. He won't let him get away."

The second terrorist was caught a few hundred metres further, in the depths of the forest, wounded in the back and in the leg. He was dragging himself along on his stomach, clutching at rocks and tree roots. Rahal placed a foot on the back of his neck, pinning him to the ground.

"Well, well, isn't he the son of Hassine the pedlar?"

"It's him all right," agreed Tahar. "We're even cousins, him and me."

Allal leaned over the terrorist, grabbed him by the hair as if to break his neck.

"Where's Sarah?"

The terrorist let out a brief laugh that made his limbs shake. He looked at the policeman, and bared his reddened teeth in a snarl:

"You won't get off lightly, cop. You're entitled to the same special treatment as the rest of your lot, I promise you."

"Where's my wife?"

"Your ex-wife, you mean. She's no longer yours, now. Tej gave her to Kada Hilal as a present. They must be having a right old good time with her now, both of them. Don't you worry about her. She's not likely to be bored. Women rarely have time to get bored out here."

"Where's the camp?" raged Mourad. "Tell me where

the camp is or I'll blow your brains out, you filthy bastard!"

"You know, you dope head, you scare me so much, I'm shitting myself."

Once again, he contracted in a spasm of laughter that shook his entire body. His head lolled, flopped to one side, and his eyes rolled upwards.

"Watch out!" cried Tahar, "He's passing out. Don't let him lose consciousness. We won't be able to bring him round."

"Leave it to me," cut in Rahal, pushing the others aside. I'll get him back on his feet again in no time."

He knelt by the terrorist and dealt him a series of resounding slaps.

"Shit! Massage his heart. We're losing him."

The terrorist gave out a sigh and went rigid. Rahal continued to shake him, but neither his insults nor his efforts succeeded in resuscitating him.

Calm seemed to have settled over the clearing once more. Despite the fierce sun, the shadow from the trees created the coolness of an oasis. Concealed among the foliage, a blackbird was singing. Sarah lay there on the downy ground. She was naked. Her blonde hair, teased by the breeze, spread out around her like a puddle of gold. Her rounded back showed whip lashes. Her wrists were bound with wire and her ankles were chained.

Standing before her, Rahal seemed to be thinking of what she had been, a few months earlier: a radiant virgin whom all the young men dreamed about. He remembered her silhouette, as delicate as a reed, but bewitching and fleeting like a mirage deep in the desert.

He slowly removed his jacket to cover the corpse. Behind him, the rest of the group stood transfixed. They stared in silence, not knowing what else to do.

Rahal meditated by Sarah's body for a moment and came back. He heard himself mutter to Allal:

"I'm so sorry."

The policeman didn't hear him. His eyes were wild. Only his lips moved in his ashen face, unable to utter the slightest sound. He remained thus for an eternity before approaching the scene of the atrocity. His legs knocked together as he staggered and swayed, making his way through a fog.

Mourad nodded and withdrew, followed by the group. Jafer stood as if turned to stone. Someone pulled him by the arm. He refused to leave.

Allal sank down by his wife's body. His trembling hand reached out to stroke her hair spread over the grass.

"Why?" he groaned.

Rahal turned around. He saw the policeman lean over his wife and pick her up . . .

"Noooo!"

Too late: a tremendous explosion threw Allal and Sarah across the clearing in an eddy of flames and flesh. Jafer was flung against a tree, his stomach split open by shrapnel. Rahal rolled into a ditch, catapulted by the force of the blast. Mourad sat up, dumbfounded. He didn't understand. Around him, four men were screaming and writhing on the ground. Another lay there, disfigured, his chest smouldering.

"What happened?" asked the panic-stricken survivors, "What happened?"

One man who had miraculously escaped wandered round and round in circles in a stupor, pointing at Sarah and Allal's bodies blown to pieces:

"The body was booby-trapped," he stammered, "her body was booby-trapped . . ."

Chapter twenty-four

The day was drawing to an end like a fallen *griot* taking his final bow. Evening lurked, ready to engulf the forest in darkness. In the sky, where not a cloud deigned to stir, infinitesimal stars went round in circles, like prayers seeking God. Something in the air was giving up the ghost. The trees lulled into drowsiness and the dogs were oblivious to the death throes. Daylight beat its retreat surrounded by indifference. It would die the same death as a rustling in the thickets, like a legend that stops as the spirit grows dull.

Dactylo was distraught. The ruins had upset him. The hand of obscurantism had wiped out their memory. Hideous breeze-block walls had usurped their majesty. Soon they would disappear beneath iron and concrete, and the hill would succumb to the rule of coarseness. All that would be left to the profaners, by way of a memento, would be the remorse of those who had endorsed the sacrilege by turning a blind eye.

Dactylo wandered among the brambles and the bitterness. He did not dare brave the desecrated valley or the scarred fields ripped apart around him. He was weary of chasing a dream across a landscape that continually drove him to despair. The worst error is a tame utopia . . . Night overtook him at the entrance to the village. His house was as welcoming as a funeral. Dactylo wasn't hungry. He just wanted to sleep. He slid into his bed and lay motionless.

"Get up, you in there!"

The public letter-writer leaped out of bed and groped for the light switch. Five armed men were standing in the room, their beards as wild as fleece, their clothes filthy and a deadly gleam in their eyes.

Tej Osmane laid his Kalashnikov next to the typewriter, perched one buttock on the corner of the table and clasped his hands around his knees.

"What are you doing in the dark, mister scholar?"

"I'm rehearsing for the eternal night and my friends' mourning."

"What makes you think we intend to harm you?"

"You don't burst in like this on the people you're fond of."

Tej sniggered.

"You've hit the nail on the head. The boss of hell needs a secretary. He sent me to recruit you."

Dactylo pushed back the cover and sat up. A terrorist nervously gripped his sawn-off shotgun. Tej calmed him down before turning round to look at the shelves laden with books.

"At the end of the day, all your reading isn't much use, is it?"

"It depends which way you want to develop."

"Is it your books that give you the strength to ignore reality? Why didn't you go home after the '62 war? Were you afraid of finding someone else in your wife's arms?"

"He's just a fool with no balls," said Zane. "He seeks in books what he's not prepared to confront in life. Don't waste any more time on him than he deserves. He's a nutter, a barmy loser. He's been saying bad things about us from the start, stirring people up against the *Mujahedin*. Slit his throat, emir. There's no other way of stopping his big mouth."

Tej rose gingerly and went over to the bookshelves. With his fingertips, he pushed the books to the floor, one by one.

"Books are man's worst enemy, Dac. They colonize your head. If there really is salvation, you must seek it within yourself. The salvation of others does not belong to you. It becomes dangerous as soon as you embrace it."

He violently knocked the bookcase over. The remaining books tumbled out and fell to the floor.

"Your books lied to you, poor fool. They whispered sweet nothings."

Then he went and looked closely at the portraits of writers hanging on the wall.

"Those fellows are nothing but frauds. They make up stories that they are incapable of living out and give their characters the parts they are unable to play . . . Writers are forgers, Dactylo, deceivers of fools. They are the first not to believe their own theories. Unfortunately, as long as idiots

191

continue to believe in their wild imaginings, they won't see any reason to stop."

He tore the portraits down and threw them in the rubbish bin.

"It's the only place they belong, after the cemetery."

He returned to the public letter-writer. Dactylo did not know how he managed to get to his feet. Fear gnawed at his guts and crippled his legs. His being was crumbling, disintegrating, yet he fought with every ounce of his shredded strength not to weaken, not to beg.

"Why don't you speak?" Zane persecuted him. "You've usually got such a way with words. What's come over you all of a sudden? What's happened to your high-flown speeches, all those long words that nobody can be bothered to decipher in the dictionary?"

Tej picked up his Kalashnikov. His lugubrious eyes darkened, and he said:

"I hate books, Dactylo. Whether they're written by poets or imams, they always make me mad. I'm allergic to the smell of paper, to their shape and to their authors' smugness. I hate being told what to do. After all, what do they know of life, what do they know of people? They barely know what they're trying to say. The world is so complex. It's impossible to pin it down, to understand all its mechanisms. Besides, you can't save the world with words. For me, writing is the prime example of representation. The only thing I believe in, is this," he added, brandishing his gun. "The gun never goes back on its word. When it lays down the law, it's final. Burn all this crap," he commanded his men. "And you, public letter-writer, stand in front. This evening you have a ringside seat at the most spectacular carnival of your miserable life."

Zane rushed out into the courtyard to fetch the jerry cans, poured petrol over the books, the bed and the curtains, and struck a match.

"Watch out fellows, say cheese. Watch the birdie."

A dazzling sheet of flame leaped up, engulfing the room. Zane retreated to the far end of the patio, his hands over his mouth to suppress a shriek of delight. He was jubilant, enthralled by the spreading inferno.

Dactylo staggered as the terrorists rained blows on him with the butts of their guns to make him advance along the track. Behind him, the flames were dancing through his house, long tentacles escaping through the windows, crackling, gushing skywards.

At the foot of the hill, a few cables' lengths away from Ghachimat, the village of Moulay Naim was also burning. Volleys of shots and explosions could be heard. The cry of the mob being attacked rang out in the night, rolled on the mountainside and came to rest deep in the forest.

"Look, Dactylo," triumphed Tej. "Look at the traitors' *douar* going up in smoke. So what happened to its self-defence group? They thought they'd frighten me with their kids. I have given orders to my men to spare neither beasts nor babies. Isn't it a wonderful sight! Listen to them howl in terror and frustration. The best thing is, there'll be no report of their deaths in tomorrow's papers. They lived anonymously, they'll die unknown to anybody, because officially they have never really counted. The wretches. They can scream all night, neither the army nor God will lift a little finger to help them. Wherever Tej Ed-Dine treads, everything perishes."

Dactylo was seized by his shirt collar and flung to the ground. He was bound. Zane squatted in front of him.

"Say something, letter-writer. Try and convince them, for goodness sake. Prove to them that they're wrong. You talk so well. Darn it, I'm really sad. I'm going to miss your lovely words. Please say something before you cop it . . . for posterity."

Dactylo closed his eyes with all his strength, and clenched his jaw. The blade brushed the end of his nose, and slid gently over his chin.

"Say something, you bastard."

He felt his body jerk under the bite of the blade. Thousands of tiny flames exploded in his head. His mouth rapidly filled with blood. His eyes were wide with pain. He saw a path leading off into the bracken, a tongue of the river licking the reeds, an empty house at the end of the path, then nothing . . . just a swirling dawn sucking him slowly towards an unknown world.

Chapter twenty-five

Smail Ich emerged from his lair, giant-like, his face hooded in a filthy fleece. He looked up at the cloudless sky then at the trees bordering the camp, and shook his head from left to right like a boxer. He wore an oilcloth apron, tied at the back with a hemp string. From his leather belt hung two butcher's knives, a flick-knife in its case and a sharpened machete. Delighted with his rig-out, he threw his head back and let out a manic laugh across the silence.

"What do you say about that?" he cried to his men around him.

He thrust his gargantuan belly forward, and smoothed his apron.

"If only someone could take a picture of me in my ceremonial dress. For posterity." He proudly jangled his murderer's arsenal. "Where's that bloody basin?"

"Here it is, Khouf Khan," someone replied.

'Smail puffed out his chest. His nickname, which made whole villages and his own companions quake, gave him an immeasurable sense of satisfaction. Since he had decapitated the imam Hadji Salah, he paraded it everywhere, like a major feat of arms.

He crouched in front of the basin, washed his hands up to the elbows – as for ablutions – splashed his face, and stood up, wiping his palms on his buttocks. Then he turned to the two prisoners. The younger was a scout leader caught during a fake road block. The other was a police officer in his fifties, a stocky man, his face marked by suffering. Kidnapped the day before, he had undergone several interrogations, but neither torture nor the promise of a secure life had succeeded in prising a scrap of information from him.

"Take the first one into the *oued*, and make sure you tie him up properly. I hate being kicked in the back."

Three followers jumped frenziedly on the young scout leader who began howling and struggling. 'Smail prolonged the agony for a few minutes before swinging round to the policeman.

"Not him, the other one . . ."

Released and half-mad, the scout leader crawled feverishly towards his place at the foot of the tree, and hunched up into a ball. The police officer was on his feet, ready to be executed. He looked 'Smail up and down and said:

"You're pathetic."

"For the moment, *taghout*, you're the one who's pathetic."

"We'll meet again, *up there*."

"Don't be so sure, cop. We won't be staying at the same address."

The officer spat on the ground:

"You're a madman!"

The three men beat him and bundled him towards the river.

"Don't damage him," shouted 'Smail. "I intend to exhibit his beautiful mug in his village square."

Sitting on a rock, his gun between his thighs, Boudjema didn't seem to be enjoying the spectacle.

A muffled murmur came from the forest. A fire crackled in the middle of the camp, while the smell of burning flesh attracted the jackals whose agitated presence in the coppice was tangible. The wind bore the sound of the crying of the women kidnapped by the mob during their punitive expeditions against the little villages. The men married them in the space of one night and after one embrace, disembowelled them. These relations were known as a marriage of enjoyment: a quick *fatihah* before fornication, and everything that followed was blessed.

'Smail's laugh rang out in the night. His silhouette briefly blocked out the filtered light of his lair and vanished into the bushes. The splashing of his urine cascaded in the darkness.

Yusef arrived with his dinner and sank down beside Boudjema, sitting alone, apart from the others. He crammed a chunk of meat into his mouth with a loud sucking noise, and licked his fingers dripping with oil.

"Usually," he said to Boudjema, "as soon as a *taghout* is brought in, you rush to intercept him so fast that your shadow can't keep up with you. What's happened to your enthusiasm?"

"Would you mind leaving me alone. I don't feel too good."

Yusef ran his tongue over his lips, caught a string of meat in his moustache, and swallowed it. He said:

"Sheikh Abbas used to say: 'Great nations have always been built on mass graves. Blood nourishes them as dung nourishes the earth.' I thought you worshipped him."

Boudjema stared intently at Yusef.

"Did Tej send you?"

"What makes you think that?"

"He's probably noticed my enthusiasm plummeting too."

"He hasn't said a word about you."

"Hey," begged the scout leader, "you're not going to kill me, are you? I haven't done anything."

Yusef threw a stone at him.

"Shut up, dog."

"I'm a scout leader. I teach the scouts botany."

"Shut up."

The leader huddled at the base of the tree and began to whimper.

"If you have a problem," said Yusef to Boudjema, "you can share it with me. We are more than brothers. Between us, we'll work it out. I'm worried about you. It's not wise to set yourself apart from the group. You're attracting attention and arousing suspicion. Many of our comrades-in-arms have been executed on the spot by 'Smail on the basis of suspicion. Some purely to serve as an example. They were as decent as the next fellow. Spy mania is raging. The slightest irregularity creates panic. Meanwhile, you carry on setting yourself apart, stupidly making yourself vulnerable. No, don't say anything. I haven't come to chat with you. I'm very fond of you. I don't want you to end up with your throat slit, that's all. Tej wouldn't spare his own father. Especially in recent times. He's out of control. So watch it. Mix in with the herd and try to keep out of his sights. And don't forget: your brother Mourad took up arms against us. If I were in your shoes, I'd be doubly careful . . ."

"Hey!" cried the scout leader again. "What use is it to you to kill me. I'm just a scout leader . . ."

"I don't believe it," groaned Yusef. "He's driving me round the bend."

"I don't want to die . . . I don't want to die . . . I-don't-want-to-di-ie . . ."

With each syllable, the scout leader banged the back of his head against the tree trunk. The terrorists paused in the middle of their meal to watch him. One of them clapped his hands to beat the rhythm and repeated after the leader:

"He-does-n't-want-to-di-ie."

The others followed suit, and began to chant:

"He-does-n't-want-to-di-ie. He-does-n't-want-to-di-ie."

Boudjema picked up his gun, and went off to stretch his legs and ease his mind by the river.

The next morning, when he went to relieve the guard,

Yusef discovered a sentry in a ditch, his legs caught in the branches and his throat slit.

The prisoner had vanished.

So had Boudjema.

The two Naaman brothers had nearly finished camouflaging the new observation post. They had dug a hole one and a half metres deep on the side of the ridge as well as a tiny furrow so they could slip behind the rock as a fallback. Najib's hands were burning. The branches he had arranged around the hole had scratched his palms raw. Dripping with sweat, his lips bloodless, he collapsed on the mound of earth he had dug up. His young brother, Chabane, a scrawny adolescent, lay under a bush, his shirt open revealing his abnormally hollow stomach. He was fanning himself with his cap, to no avail.

Najib raised the flask to his lips, then he sprinkled his neck and the top of his scabby head.

"You should have brought your medicine with you," he said.

"I barely had time to escape over the rooftops."

"This time, *they* are determined. *They* won't let us get away. We can't go back, and we can't slip past them. Boudjema must have co-operated with them all the way. He didn't forget a single detail, the bastard. I wonder whether I did the right thing in dragging you into this shitty mess."

"What's done is done."

"I'm really worried about your lungs. You're not strong enough."

Chabane let his cap fall over his face.

"You can't escape destiny, big brother. Don't feel guilty. I'm seventeen, you know. I can take responsibility for myself."

In the white-hot sky above the valley, helicopters flew low, skimming the hilltops like dragonflies. Intermittent artillery fire caused bursts of fire and smoke in the forest. An impressive military convoy snaked along the road to Moulay Naim, while other units that had been deployed for two days marched into the surrounding villages carrying out a major search operation.

"You shouldn't have joined us," said Najib, sounding stressed.

"There were road blocks everywhere. I had no choice."

Najib was pained at the sight of his brother with his sickly chest, swarthy complexion and eyes sunk deep in his furrowed brow.

Since Boudjema's desertion, the *katiba* had been in constant retreat towards the mountain heights. They had mined the tracks with home-made bombs to hamper the progress of the army, but the soldiers, cleverly deployed, were advancing fast, inflicting heavy losses on them with each clash.

"Curse you, Boudjema," fulminated Chabane. "You can't take it with you to Paradise."

Najib smiled bitterly:

"We've left Paradise behind. The long evening gatherings, the weddings in the balmy nights, the joking on every street corner, the girls we spied on around the *marabouts*, do you remember? The songs of the old woman on the coping of the well, the mood swings of the old man, Issa-the-disgrace's

absent-mindedness, the troubadours, the braying of the donkeys in the heat of the afternoon . . . that was paradise, the
true paradise, *ours*, as easy as falling off a log. It's behind us
now. Don't look at me like that, kid. We've been duped, like
fools. They wound us up like alarm-clocks and let us ring a
twenty-fifth hour that is completely out of step."

"You're not going to tell me that we killed all those
people for nothing?"

Najib puffed out his cheeks. His gaze went back to the
advancing convoys.

"It's the truth."

Chabane was devastated by his elder brother's diatribe.
His hand faltered before grabbing Najib's.

"What are we going to do?"

"You're going to get out of here. Your age will be a
point in your favour."

"What about you?"

"My name's on all the wanted lists. I haven't got a
chance."

"Give yourself up."

"It's too late."

"I won't leave without you."

Najib grasped his brother's shoulders:

"You're going to clear off, and now. No embraces, no
fuss. There's a goat track just after the forest post. You have one
chance in a hundred of reaching it safely, and you're going to
try. The terrain is uneven. On the other side of the hill, there's
an abandoned farm. Hide in the surrounding orchards, at night.
In the morning, make your way to the road and give yourself
up. As for me, I'll try to find a way out, I promise you."

Chabane did not press matters. When the elder commands, the younger obeys. He put his flask, a can of food and a pistol in his kit bag. Najib turned his back, meaningfully.

"Take care of yourself, big brother."

"Get out of here."

Chabane contemplated his cap sadly, pulled it down over his ears and rushed down the path, grasping the bushes for support.

The helicopters were getting closer. Najib slid into the hole and covered it with the foliage. At that precise moment, in the depths of the gloom, he became aware of the extent of his solitude.

'Smail Ich took aim at the helicopter. The machine was so close that he could see its blades stirring up the air. A whistle rent the sky. The observation post flew up in a whirl of dust and flames. The artillery fired mercilessly at the ridge. Najib emerged from the smoke, staggering, his arms blown off. Two helicopters appeared above the woods. Their rockets shattered the surroundings. A fire started in the forest and spread to the copse in a whirling trail. 'Smail came out into the open. His feet firmly planted, he thumped his chest with his fist, grinning maniacally. He was felled by an explosion, landing on his back, his eyes bulging, his mouth wide open in a stricken laugh. The first cordon of soldiers rapidly rushed into the copse amid a volley of gunfire. The helicopters withdrew and the artillery transferred its fire to the ridges to prevent the *katiba* from retreating.

*   *   *

The whole of Ghachimat was looking in the direction of the mountain. Perched on the terraces, their hands shading their eyes, the women scrutinized the horizon. In the village square, the children were riveted to the spot in bewilderment. The Elders and the men stood along the hilltop, some straddling donkeys, others leaning on walking sticks. They followed the incessant aerobatics of the helicopters leaving dark trails. The bombing sent up clouds of birds across the plain.

Hadji Menouar rolled up the hem of his robe over his old calves covered in mosquito bites. An irrepressible joy deformed his features.

"Listen to that. It's music to our ears," he said, jerking his thumb towards the theatre of operations. "Evil will always remain an unrepentant fool. Now we'll see whether they've really got any guts or not, those murderers of babes."

Hadji Baroudi nodded his head. His false teeth were about to leap out of his mouth. Grinning from ear to ear, he jumped up and down at the sound of the explosions.

"That'll shut them up once and for all."

"And about time too," grumbled an old man.

"Better late than never," retorted Zane. "We were beginning to despair."

"Well, I didn't like those fellows from the beginning," boasted a mountain-dweller, absent-mindedly bruising his donkey's ears. "You could see from their rotten faces that it was going to end up badly: not a smile, not a kind word. They were mad, even in their sleep. They lashed out without thinking. The only favour fellows like that can do their neighbour is to die. All they do is kill and destroy."

Zane nodded and clapped energetically.

A swarm of mosquitoes buzzed around the street lamp. It was past midnight. The fires raging through the forests of Djebel El-Khouf intensified the heat of the night. Zane couldn't sleep. Sprawled on a mattress on the veranda, he stared pensively at the patio door. In the distance, sporadic detonations rang out like false notes amid the chirring. Ghachimat was holding its breath. Ghachimat didn't know what else to do. It lived with its claustrophobia.

But Zane was calm. What he lacked in size, he made up for in cunning. He would always be able to negotiate his fortunes depending on the circumstances. He turned on his back and clasped his hands over his podgy stomach, proud of his nascent paunch. In the sky, playful stars winked at him. One looked as if it was having more fun than the others. Zane was sure that was his star.

There was a knock at the door. Without hesitating, Zane went to open it. A body fell on him, knocking him over. He kicked it away and braced himself against the wall to free himself, cursing the blood on his hands and his robe.

The man on the ground was wounded. He was dying.

"That's all I needed," grumbled the dwarf, recognizing Tej Osmane.

The latter tried to lean on his gun, grabbed at the door but was unable to get up.

"Get me out of here," he groaned.

Calmly, as though he did this every day, the dwarf first moved the Kalashnikov out of the emir's reach, removed the magazine, activated the breech to remove the bullet, laid the whole thing on the coffee table and leaned over Tej.

"You've got at least five big chunks of metal in your gut," he stated. "No way you'll be partying tonight."

"Go and get Doctor Driss."

"Driss is an excellent vet, but he isn't God. I don't see how he can fix you up."

"Please, don't waste time," panted Tej feverishly.

"Moulay Naim's surrounded."

"Find a way . . ."

Worn out by the effort of shouting, Tej vacillated for a moment before getting a fresh grip on himself. He made a superhuman effort to sit up, leaned against the wall, ashen and shivering, and closed his eyes to recuperate. Zane opened his jacket to examine his wounds.

"Hum, nasty, very nasty . . ."

"The doctor, quick . . ."

Zane had to move his ear close to the dying man's mouth to catch his words.

"Right away, boss, right away. Now just try not to bleed all over my floor and make a mess."

Zane pretended to go out in search of the doctor. Once in the street, he sat down on the pavement, lit a cigarette and thought about what he should do. After a few long drags, he decided to do nothing at all. He calmly finished his cigarette, counted the stars and then counted them again, then went back to the wounded man.

"I've sent someone to fetch him," he lied, sitting on

the table. "There's no danger, he's a sympathizer. Driss will be here in under half an hour."

Tej thanked him with a slight nod. His dying eyes lingered on the gaping lumpy wounds in his chest, and sought those of the dwarf, who was much more preoccupied with examining his fingernails than with the blood beginning to spread over the floor.

"What time is it?"

"Dunno."

"Approximately?"

"Maybe one a.m., maybe nearly two. Are you expecting someone?"

"The doctor . . ."

"There are road blocks everywhere."

Tej fluttered his eyelids.

"I can't see very well."

"It must be the beginning of a squint. You've been looking at things lopsidedly for such a long time."

"I'm cold. Give me a blanket."

"You don't need one. How many survivors?"

Tej didn't have enough breath to reply.

"None."

Tej acquiesced with his eyes.

"That was predictable. In Ghachimat, nobody had any illusions. Seeing they sent a whole armada to get you, we didn't rate your chances very high. It's a miracle you're still hanging around here."

Tej wasn't aware of the note of sarcasm in the dwarf's words. He hunched over his wounds, listening for the slightest creak in the hope that the doctor had arrived.

"He won't come," announced Zane swinging his legs.
Tej frowned.

Zane explained:

"Driss won't come. I didn't send anybody to fetch him."

"What does that mean?"

Zane climbed on the table and squatted on his haunches, his hands crossed on his knees.

"When I was a kid, I always sat like this on the roof of our shack. I could stay in this position for hours. My mother thought I looked like a frozen little sparrow. That wasn't quite right. I wanted to be a vulture. I watched the village from up on my perch like a bird of prey eyeing its quarry. I already knew, at that age without any real excuses, that I had been born with the patience of a predator, that however long my prey managed to survive, it would end up coming to die at my feet. And here you are, Tej Osmane, son of Issa-the-disgrace. *At my feet.*"

Tej didn't quite follow the dwarf's words. He thought he was delirious.

Zane flapped his wings like a vulture before it goes rigid, curiously hieratic, a claw-like hand in front of his mouth to make a beak like a bird of prey's. He was aware of the resonance of each of his words, of the balance of each of his movements. His puffed-out cheeks began to quiver spasmodically. His lips formed a series of hate-filled grimaces. His voice found a passage through his guts, burst from his throat in a rush of bile and hit Tej with the force of vomit:

"We were two rejected kids, Tej. You bore your father's disgrace, I that of the midget. Gods and men drove us to distraction. We were two very different creatures, two sick freaks rejected by everyone. You needed someone. I thought I was that person, and I hoped, in exchange, that you would be that someone for me. Together, we would be able to support each other, you the *vile beast* and me the *fairground beast*. But you let me down. You weren't my ally. You were worse than the others, Tej. You used me like an old rag. You made me wear a *gandoura* all year round, even in summer, and you dragged me to the souks so you could slip the fruit you stole into my hood. When we got caught, you pointed at me and protested, while I got beaten. When we got away, you grabbed all the booty and didn't even leave me a stalk. I told myself that eventually you'd settle down. But you haven't changed a bit. You've carried on using me, betraying me, destroying my pride. I was your beast of burden, your scapegoat, your underdog, and you've no idea how much I've hated you."

"We were kids, Zane."

"Exactly. We were kids, weak and wretched, so little and so vulnerable, unable to defend ourselves and unable to understand. If you haven't forgiven, how do you expect me to forgive?"

"That's ridiculous. I couldn't know, at the time. Maybe I was mean to you, but I didn't realize it, I promise you. I didn't know how to love. I didn't know the meaning of love. For the rest, it's not the same. I'm not taking revenge, no; I'm fighting for an ideal . . ."

"Tsst! Tsst! I'm not one of your followers. Don't kid me. Men like you and me don't have ideals. Mere pretexts act as triggers. I'm convinced you don't even believe in God."

Tej was choking. His flailing hands clawed at the ground and were grazed.

"Think what I've made you now: the fortune I've helped you amass, the house, the land, the bakery . . ."

Zane sniggered contemptuously:

"Do you know why dwarves are little, Tej? It's because they spend more time plotting than they do growing. I've known you were a winner from the beginning. I staked my future on you. You were my Solomon's ring, I twisted you around my finger at my whim. A pawn, that's all you've been for me. As Kada Hilal was for you. Now I've finished with you, I'm going to have to get rid of your carcase."

Tej tried to get up. His last strength was ebbing away. He fell back against the wall, his heart wild, his face tortured.

"You're dead, Tej. You're already beginning to stink."

"What are you going to do?"

"There's a price on your head. I've got to pocket the reward, at the very least. The rest will take care of itself. Tomorrow, they'll be one name on everyone's lips: Zane, the heroic Zane, slayer of Osmane Tej Ed-Dine, caliph of the Apocalypse."

"I thought you were on my side."

"This is a democracy, darling: everyone *has a duty* to look after their own interests."

"Cur!" gurgled Tej.

"What have you got against curs, son of Issa-the-disgrace? They don't have any prejudices, dogs don't. They may be our best friends, but we still lock them up in kennels and expect them to guard our homes. It's because we've never deserved them that we don't deserve to be treated any better than them."

Tej leaned his head against the wall and let out a wail.

His eyes grew wild, his neck jerked in a final spasm and his gaze faltered as a trickle of blood ran down from the corner of his mouth. He slid slowly onto his side and moved no more.

From the top of his perch, Zane puffed out his chest and prepared to spread his vulture's wings over the body lying at his feet.

Glossary

Astaghfiru 'llah: "I ask for God's forgiveness"

caid: governor

djebel: hill

douar: village

emir: military commander

fellah (pl. *fellahin*): a peasant

fatihah: the short first sura of the Koran, used by Muslims as a prayer.

fatwa: a religious decree issued by a Muslim leader.

FIS: Front Islamique du Salut (Islamic Salvation Front)

gandoura: tunic

GIA: Groupe Islamique Armé (Armed Islamic Group)

griot: a class of travelling poets, musicians, and entertainers in North and West Africa, whose duties include the recitation of tribal and family histories; an oral folk-historian or village story-teller, a praise-singer. Griots are reputed to be in touch with the spirits.

Hadith: the body of traditions relating to Muhammad, which now form a supplement to the Koran, called the Sunna.

Hadji: the title given to a man/woman who has made the pilgrimage to Mecca.

Hamza: the Prophet's uncle. Great warrior of Islam.

harki: Muslim irregulars, trained and armed by the SAS, who fought with the French in the War of Independence and subsequently received French nationality.

hijab: veil

Houbel: pre-Islamic Mecca god

Iblis: Satan

imam: officiating priest of a Muslim mosque

jellabah: a smock-like garment

Jihad: "Struggle"; a religious war of Muslims against unbelievers in Islam, inculcated as a duty by the Koran and traditions.

kamis: loose shirt

katiba: squadron

Lalla: title given to a princess

litham: a cloth veil wound round the head leaving only the eyes uncovered and worn by the men of the Tuareg people of the central Sahara desert.

Majlis: Fundamentalists' consultative assembly

maquisard: guerilla fighters during the War of Independence, 1954–1962

marabout: a Muslim hermit or monk, particularly amongst the Arabs and Berbers of North Africa.

Mehdi (the imam of salvation): a messianic imam who would

come back to make men observe God's Word and save humanity from the forces of evil.

minbar: pulpit

Mujahed (pl. *Mujahedin*): one who fights in a *Jihad* or holy war in Islamic countries: freedom fighters; now specifically fundamentalist Muslims who use guerilla warfare to assert their claims.

oued: river

pasha: officer of high rank, military commanders, or governors of provinces.

Raïs: President

SAS: Section Administrative Spécialisée (Specialist Administrative Section) of the French army, created in 1955 to establish contact with the Muslim population and weaken nationalist influence in rural areas.

Sunna: the body of traditional sayings and customs attributed to Muhammad and supplementing the Koran.

taghout: despot

About the author

Mohammed Moulessehoul

Yasmina Khadra is the pseudonym of the Algerian author Mohammed Moulessehoul, who was born in 1956. A high ranking officer in the Algerian army, he went into exile in France in 2000 where he now lives in seclusion. In his several writings on the civil war in Algeria, Khadra exposes the current regime and the fundamentalist opposition as the joint guilty parties in the Algerian Tragedy.

Before his admission of identity in 2001, a leading critic in France wrote: "A he or a she? It doesn't matter. What matters is that Yasmina Khadra is today one of Algeria's most important writers.'

The fonts used in this book are from the Garamond and Meta families.